THE JOY OF US

USA TODAY BESTSELLING AUTHOR

KENNEDY FOX

Copyright © 2022 Kennedy Fox
www.kennedyfoxbooks.com

The Joy of Us
Love in Isolation, #6

Cover designer: Outlined with Love Designs
Cover image: Lindee Robinson Photography
Copy editor: Editing 4 Indies

LOVE IN ISOLATION SERIES READING ORDER

The Two of Us
Elijah & Cameron
Brother's best friend, forced proximity romance

The Best of Us
Ryan & Kendall
Best friend's brother, snowed-in, forced proximity romance

The End of Us
Tristan & Piper
Forbidden bodyguard, forced proximity romance

The Heart of Us
Easton & Tatum
Reverse age gap, forced proximity romance

The Fall of Us
Finn & Oakley
Grumpy/sunshine, fake dating, forced proximity romance

The Joy of Us
Levi & Fallon
Reverse grumpy/sunshine, forced proximity romance

Whenever you're closed off
I'ma kick in the door to your heart
Whenever your head's down
I'll be the light in your darkest night
I'ma make you a promise
I will give you my love and I won't hold back

"Love Me"
-Stanaj

CHAPTER ONE

FALLON

DAY 1

As SOON AS the plane lands at the small connecting airport, I grab my
carry-on and laptop bag. I look at the monitor with my upcoming flight so
I can find my gate and see DELAYED next to it.

"*Dammit,*" I mutter and suck in a deep breath. My first flight was
already delayed, and I feel that this one might get canceled because of the
heavy snowfall.

I open my weather app and see a storm hovering on the radar.
Annoyed, I grab my suitcase and make my way across the tiny airport. It's
a quarter to three, and my patience is already waning.

I left my apartment around four this morning so I could arrive before
dark since there's a three-hour time difference between Seattle and
Vermont.

Just out of curiosity, I check to see how far from the airport the rental
property my assistant, Peggy, booked for me was. Right now, my choices
are to drive a couple of hours in a near whiteout or potentially be stuck in
this airport overnight.

I mull it over for ten minutes before calling my sister, Taryn. She's two
years older and always has good advice. She might not understand my

1

dating issues and being single, considering she's been with the same man since she was sixteen, but most of her other suggestions are spot-on.

"Hey! Did you make it?" Taryn asks as soon as she answers.

I blow out a frustrated breath. "No. The flight is delayed, and I think it's gonna get canceled. I checked the radar, and the weather doesn't look promising. I've flown enough to know they won't fly in this."

"Tell me you're not going to rent a car and drive the rest of the way," she mutters.

"I was thinking about it," I admit.

She sighs. "I know you too well. Please be careful. I don't want anything to happen to you."

A sad smile touches my lips because it's that time of year we both dread—Christmas. "I'm always careful. I promise."

I weigh my odds and decide to check if any rental vehicles are available. If there aren't, then I'll just wait.

As I make my way across the airport, I glance at each TV to see if anything has changed. It hasn't.

The car rental line snakes around the corner, so it'll be a miracle if I'm not turned away.

"Looks like they canceled all the outgoing flights for the day," an older woman behind me says as more people join our line. It nearly triples in size.

"Really? Great." I shake my head, knowing this is my only chance to get the hell out of here.

When it's finally my turn, the woman asks if I have a reservation.

"No. Do you have anything available? Price doesn't matter," I explain, pulling out my company credit card.

She taps away on the keyboard and frowns. "Hmm. It doesn't look like we do. Hold on one second, though. I need to check something."

The woman offers a small smile before stepping away. Although it's cold from the doors constantly opening and closing, I'm sweating bullets as I wait for her to return.

If I could go back in time to when my boss reassigned this project, I'd have begged him to choose someone else. Writing a piece on Vermont's most famous Christmas small town and the traditions from an outsider's perspective was only slightly better than interviewing dog owners about their favorite pet sweaters. Both make me want to gouge my eyes out with a fork, but when a co-worker got a bad case of the flu, I sympathized and took it.

Once my assistant confirmed my travel plans, it was a done deal. I was actually looking forward to being secluded in a winter wonderland on the company's dime. Now, it feels like a mistake.

To make matters worse, the most annoying song with jingle bells blares over the loudspeaker. I'm regretting every decision in my life that brought me here.

"So we do have *one* vehicle left, but it's a minivan. Would you like it?"

"A *minivan*?" I groan.

She nods, waiting patiently for my answer. Not my first choice, but then again, do I even have a damn choice? I don't even care at this point. I just want out of here.

"I'll take it," I tell her reluctantly.

The woman grins. "Good thing, because I think everyone behind you would probably kill for it. Bonus, it has satellite radio and heated seats."

"Thank you," I offer, truly thankful.

She slides the keys toward me and types up my contract. I get full insurance and prepay for fuel, then I'm on my *unmerry* way. I grab my shit and head outside. The van looks filthy, but I don't have room to complain.

I climb inside, and holiday music blares as soon as I crank it. "I think the fuck not." I turn it off, then blast the heat. I already can't escape this damn holiday, and I know it will just get worse.

Before taking off, I plug in the address to the rental cabin and know it'll take longer than the two hours it estimates.

I take it slow to avoid driving into a ditch. I'm not used to this amount of snow, so I can only see a couple of feet in front of me. My stress level shoots up to level eleven. There's no way I can turn around now.

I'm as committed to this drive as I am to writing this ridiculous article. The windshield wipers whoosh back and forth, and though I have them on high, they don't clear the flurries fast enough. My heart rapidly beats, and I take in slow, calm breaths, not allowing my anxiety to get the best of me.

I grip the steering wheel through the twisting curves and long straight roads.

I can't believe I'm driving a fucking minivan in a blizzard.

When I finally arrive at the infamous Vermont town, I'm drained. Some of the buildings are decorated like gingerbread houses, and colorful lights adorn all the trees and streetlights. It looks like a mini North Pole, something one would expect to see on a movie set. Santa's workshop, along with a massive tree, is the main focus in the center of the square. I continue forward, surprised to see so many people shopping.

My cabin is another twenty miles. Eventually, I turn onto a road that leads to only God knows where. Snow weighs down the branches of the evergreens lining each side of the path. The ice crunches beneath the tires, and when I arrive at a two-story cabin, my mouth drops.

I double-check the address and instructions Peggy emailed me. It's gorgeous and secluded, far enough away from town not to be in the middle of the chaos. It's about a twenty-minute drive there and back.

Once I turn off the engine, I grab everything because I only want to make one trip. By some miracle, I make it to the back deck without busting my ass. I look under the mat for the key and frown when it's not there. *What the hell?* I search for a note or a rock that it could be hiding under, but no such luck.

You've gotta be kidding me.

Instead of leaving, I try the door handle and am relieved and shocked when I find it's unlocked.

Thank God.

Slowly, I twist and push, almost expecting someone to jump out at me. The fact this place was unlocked is odd and makes me paranoid.

"Hello?" I call out. When no one answers, I sigh in relief and remove my scarf. I pull out my self-defense keychain from my pocket, then hang my coat on a spare hook by the door. My jeans are cold and wet from the snow, so after I kick off my boots, I bend and roll them up.

With rentals, the owners usually leave a binder with things to do in town or some sort of housewarming note, but I don't see anything like that. When I go into the kitchen, I notice a bowl, spoon, and coffee mug in the sink.

Opening the fridge and freezer, I see containers with leftovers and lots of frozen meat. The pantry is full of food too. I find it somewhat odd, but I'm not one to be picky, given my situation. I'll have Peggy inform them that their cleaner missed a few things before I checked in.

When I enter the living room, my eyes land on the tall Christmas tree decorated with bright colored lights and what looks like homemade Christmas ornaments. I take two steps forward, my lips pursing with distaste. I should've told Peggy to specify no holiday decorations, but I also didn't expect it to look like the inside of a Christmas store.

As I walk past the mantel, I glance over at a mini scene that looks identical to the gingerbread houses in town. I turn one of the reindeer to get a better look at its face. Whoever owns this place is weirdly obsessed. My best guess is an older couple uses this as their vacation home and rents it during the winter. They probably go by Mr. and Mrs. Claus.

Shaking my head, I grip the handle of my suitcase and carry it upstairs. I walk down a hallway, looking into each of the rooms. The largest bedroom has a king-sized bed and a fireplace. And of course, another tree decorated to the max. As I turn my head, I notice an en suite with a large tub and standing shower that I'm claiming as mine for the next two weeks. The spare room down the hall is spacious and nice, but I could go without the tree in the corner. I'm tempted to unplug every single one of them, but I don't have the energy. I'm exhausted and sore from sitting for so long.

Next year, I don't care who gets the flu, I'm not leaving Seattle in December unless it ends up with me on a beach sipping a mai tai.

I return to the large room, throw my suitcase on the bed, and grab my toiletries. I fill the tub and soak for a solid twenty minutes. Once I'm clean and dressed, I grab my laptop, place some things on the nightstand, then climb into bed. Before I check my email, I text my sister.

> FALLON
>
> Made it in one piece.

"*Barely,*" I mutter to myself.

I send her a picture of my joggers and my feet in fluffy socks.

> TARYN
>
> Why don't you light that fireplace?

> FALLON
>
> Uh, it's not gas, and I don't see any wood. And no way am I playing lumberjack in this weather.

TARYN

Glad you made it okay. Is that a Christmas tree in the bedroom?

FALLON

Unfortunately. 😕

FALLON

The whole place is decorated like a department store. It's weird.

TARYN

Maybe you'll end up leaving that place loving Christmas again. 😉

FALLON

Doubt it. But anyway, I'm gonna get some work done, then go to sleep so I can start working first thing in the morning.

TARYN

What time is it there?

FALLON

Just after six.

TARYN

Don't work too hard. Hope you get some decent sleep.

FALLON

Yes, Mama Bear. Night, sis.

I smirk at the nickname I gave her a long time ago because she's so overprotective. And still is to this day. Taryn doesn't care that I'm an independent, thirty-year-old woman, I'll always be her kid sister.

Just as I start sorting through emails and am about to reply to one of Peggy's, I hear a dog barking downstairs, along with muffled speech.

What the hell?

Did I forget to lock the door behind me?

The hair on my arms stands up as I grab my pepper spray. I look around, wondering if I can quickly slide under the bed. The closet is across the room, and I nearly stop breathing as I try to hear what's going on. Paws race up the stairs, and they're followed by heavy footsteps. Before I can scream, the door swings open, and a naked six-foot mountain man stands in front of me, looking as confused as I feel.

I inspect his dark hair and scruffy facial hair as his piercing blue eyes meet mine with horror. My gaze roams down his muscular body, seeing all of him, and panic continues as he steps toward me.

That's when I scream and pull the safety from my pepper spray.

This *cannot* be happening.

CHAPTER TWO

LEVI

SINCE ONE OF the biggest storms of the season is supposed to hit this evening, I spend most of the day helping my parents at our Christmas tree farm. After I chop a fuckton of wood for them, I go to my twin sister Lucy's house and do the same for her.

"Thanks, bro!" She waves, already dressed in her pajamas.

I look at my watch. "It's barely four."

"So? It's a pre-snow day." She shrugs. "Thanks again for the wood."

"Welcome. Couldn't let ya freeze. Check in with me after the blizzard passes," I tell her, knowing I need to get home to do the same. "Come on, Dasher," I say as my golden retriever begs to go inside with her.

"He wants to stay with me," she teases. "It's because he likes me more." She pets him, bending down and kissing his head.

"Dasher!" I whistle. He bolts toward me, hopping through the snow, making sure he's wet and filthy before getting in the truck. I give my sister a wave, then drive the couple of miles to my place.

The temperature is steadily dropping, and over the next few days, we'll get pounded with over twenty inches of snow along with harsh winds. Most of the town and grocery stores have already shut down. I actually enjoy winter storms and being stuck inside with Dasher. It's Mother Nature's way of making me rest during one of the busiest times of the year. While it might slightly hurt profits, it'll pick up again, and we'll be swamped once we reopen. Last-minute tree buyers aren't that uncommon.

Once I'm home, I park my truck on the side of the house closest to my shed. Dasher gets out and chases a rabbit to the edge of the woods, and I have to yell at him to come back. He does, then I unlock the back door, grabbing him a few treats for being a good boy on the farm today. Once he's gobbled them up, we go out to the shed to start working. All my extra wood is stored here, and I chop it year-round to keep it stocked for winter.

I keep a small heater on the floor in here for him while I work. Dasher loves the snow and cold, but he's also a baby and likes to be warm. As soon as I turn it on, he lies in front of it, watching me with his big eyes.

"This won't take me long," I explain to him as I grab my axe and chop the trunks into smaller, more manageable chunks. While my house runs off propane, I still use the fireplace.

Thirty minutes pass, and I take a quick break. My muscles are fatigued from chopping most of the day. Dasher stares at me, and I chuckle. He's just as ready as I am to go in and relax.

As I look out across the pond in front of my house, I can see the blizzard moving in. Visibility is terrible. I'm not sure how long I'll be snowed in, but I plan to catch up on some sleep. Then after it passes, I'll be on plow duty. Once I've caught my breath, I continue until I'm finally finished.

"Okay, boy. Let's go."

I turn off the small heater, then grab an armful of wood to carry inside. Dasher leads the way, and as soon as I turn the knob, he sniffs around and starts barking.

I place the logs in a small stack next to the fireplace and notice one of the reindeer in my town scene on the mantel is turned the wrong way. Making a face, I move it back to where it was.

Dasher races upstairs, still barking his head off as I undress on my way to the shower. I'll deal with my wet-ass dog after.

I slip off my jeans, push my boxers down, and open my bedroom door, naked. Unbeknownst to me, a woman lies in my bed.

I make eye contact with her as Dasher rushes forward. Quickly, I try to cover myself, not particularly wanting this stranger to see my dick, but I have more questions than answers. Neither of us knows what the fuck is going on. I try to say something, anything, but she screams in horror. She grabs something next to her, then points it at me. Everything happens so fast that I barely have time to react. Pepper spray shoots across the room and hits me directly in my eyes.

"Fuck! You just maced me!" I stumble back, trip over something hard, and fall on my ass.

"I'm calling the police!" she shrieks as Dasher sniffs me and continues to bark at the woman.

I press my palms into my face as the burn gets worse. "Please do! Tell them you broke in, then assaulted me!"

"Broke into *your* house? I don't think so. The last thing I'm going to do is let some man murder me in the middle of nowhere."

I wish I could look at her, but my eyes are stinging so fucking bad that I can only wait it out. She starts coughing, which means she probably got some residuals from the spray.

"What are you talking about, woman?"

"I'm talking about how you just broke into my rental."

"Listen to me!" My voice booms as tears roll down my cheeks. I have no idea what the fuck she's talking about.

"Ugh! Get your filthy dog off me." I can hear the mattress squeak and know he jumped on the bed.

"Dasher." I snap my fingers. "Downstairs."

I hear a thump followed by the pads of his feet trotting as he makes his way to the bottom floor. "I'd love to keep having this ridiculous conversation with you, but I really need to rinse my eyes." They feel like they're melting out of my skull.

I manage to gain my footing while keeping one hand over my junk.

"Maybe I should've tased you instead."

"I'll deal with you when I get out of the shower," I state.

"Fine!" she snaps. "But you touch me, I'll call 911 immediately."

Carefully, I take blind steps toward my bathroom. Once I'm at the sink, I spend fifteen minutes splashing cold water on my face to dilute the capsaicin she attacked me with.

Then I immediately get in the shower and wash every part of my body with soap to try to break down the oils from the spray. I stand under the stream, letting it run over my sore muscles, annoyed that I'm dealing with this bullshit.

I've lived here all my life and know almost everyone in the area, and she's definitely not a local.

After I rinse off, I get dressed and notice her shampoo, conditioner, and sea breeze-scented body wash is on the edge of my tub. She fully helped herself to my house while I was gone. Guess I'm going to have to start locking my door.

Once I've composed myself, I walk into my room, where she's still sitting cross-legged on my bed with her laptop. She quickly grabs her pepper spray when she hears me.

"Do *not* do that again."

"Or what?"

I don't have time for these games. "Who are you, and what the hell are you doing in my house?" I finally ask. Though more specifically, *my bed*.

She narrows her beautiful green eyes at me as if *I'm* the intruder. Then stands a good five feet from me.

"I'm Fallon Joy, a journalist for a magazine based in Seattle. I'm writing a center page article about this town and rented this place for two weeks while I'm here." She grabs her phone, then shows me the itinerary along with photos of the outside of my house. That smirk, paired with her confidence, tells me she believes she's proved her point.

I meet her gaze. "Well, *Fallon Joy*..." I repeat her name and chuckle at the irony.

"What's funny?"

"The fact that your last name is *Joy*, and you seem anything but joyful."

Her lips purse into a line so tight, it looks painful.

"Anyway, I'm Levi White, and my family has owned this property well before either of us was alive. I'd say it's nice to meet you, but—"

"Why did you put this cabin on a vacation rental site if you weren't going to vacate?"

"I didn't. I've never rented it out."

"So this listing isn't your cabin?"

"It is, but *I* didn't list it."

"Is this some kind of scam? You take all my money, then kick me out as soon as I get here?"

Her accusatory tone annoys me even more.

"Look up *White's Christmas Tree Farm,* and you'll see I'm not lying. Go ahead. I'll wait," I taunt, crossing my arms over my broad chest.

"Well, *Levi,*" she mimics my tone, spitting out my name like it's poison. "My assistant booked this reservation, and I've already seen the charge on my card. There must've been some sort of miscommunication with the website," she continues to run her mouth.

"Please tell me you're not that naïve. You were *scammed.* Someone put my cabin up on that website, stole your money, and left us to figure it out."

"That's not possible."

"Go to the listing now and see if it's still there. A hundred bucks says it's gone."

She furiously types on her phone. When the color drains from her face and her nostrils flare, I'm convinced she might self-destruct. I've never seen someone get worked up so quickly. But I try to give her the benefit of the doubt because I'm sure this is stressful for her, too.

"Motherfucker," she mutters, inhaling a deep breath as if she's contemplating throwing her phone out the window.

"I'm sorry someone took advantage, but you can see I'm telling the truth. This happens in touristy towns sometimes."

She gives me an unamused death glare. "*Great.* I'll just grab my things and leave. I'm sure I can find another place."

"Actually, I don't think that's a good idea right now. It's a full-on blizzard out there, and the road conditions are probably bad in this whiteout. You can sleep in my guest bedroom tonight. There's a bathroom down the hall you can use, too. We'll figure out what to do in the morning."

"Fine."

She slams her laptop shut, picks up her phone and weapons, and snatches the handle to her suitcase. Without saying another word, she storms off. Seconds later, a door slams shut, and I think she locks it.

Shaking my head, I call Dasher up to give him a quick bath. As I scrub soap over his back and belly, I think about the crazy events that just happened and wonder how the hell I'm going to navigate having a stranger in my house.

When I woke up this morning, the last thing I expected to find was a beautiful woman in my bed who thought I was there to kill her.

Who knows, with her salty attitude, I just might want to before she leaves.

CHAPTER THREE

FALLON

DAY 2

I WAKE from a dreamless sleep without an alarm. I'm not a morning person by any means—I actually *hate* mornings—but I'm an early riser. I swear my internal clock syncs with the sun no matter where I am in the world.

Once I slide out of bed, I open the curtain to see everything covered with a blanket of white. If it weren't for bad luck, I'd have none.

After I go through my morning routine and get dressed, I check my phone to see if Peggy responded to the strongly worded email I sent last night.

It sends me into a tailspin of rage when I realize she hasn't. I'm tired of her making mistakes like this, especially ones that put me in a dangerous situation. Because of her, I'm now in an uncomfortable position with a strange man.

With my phone tightly in my grip, I go downstairs and call Peggy. I don't care about the time difference. Not when she's responsible for my predicament.

"Peggy," I bark out when she finally picks up.

"You realize it's four in the morning, right?"

"I don't give a shit. Did you read my email?"

"Um…no." I hear scrambling as if she's reaching for her computer.

I groan and explain what happened. She makes a few excuses and tries to get out of this being her fault, but I interrupt her.

"I went to the website myself. It was obvious that it was a phishing site. Half the page was filled with ads and porn pop-ups. And now, I'm stuck staying at a strange man's house in the middle of a snowstorm. Not to mention, my card has to be canceled. When I checked the statement last night, it contained several charges I didn't make."

"I'm so sorry," she says. I know she's being genuine, but this was a dumb mistake, even for her. "I looked everywhere, and that was the only rental available within a fifty-mile radius."

I let out a long sigh, my heart racing over how worked up I am. "*Take. Care. Of. It.*"

Once the words leave my mouth, I end the call. As I set my phone down on the counter, I groan.

A chuckle rings out behind me, and I glare at Levi. His dog trots toward me, but I ignore him.

"Where do you keep the coffee?" I ask around a yawn.

"I don't have any."

"Seriously? Who doesn't drink coffee? Or at least have some stocked for guests?"

He lifts his finger and points at himself, then gives me a smile, one I don't return. "I didn't realize I'd have an uninvited guest." Before I can ask about getting some, he adds, "But I have hot cocoa and apple cider. That's about it. Oh, wait. I might have…"

He moves past me and opens the pantry, then digs around. A few seconds later, he sets a rusted can on the counter. "This."

I pick it up and read the label.

"This is instant, and it expired five years ago." I blink hard, hoping I'll wake up from this horrible nightmare.

"You do what you can with whatcha got. Enjoy." He smirks and then puts a kettle on the stove.

I suck in a deep breath, then snatch up my phone because I won't function properly without some caffeine. "Fine. I'll just get some delivered."

A roar of a laugh escapes him. "Sweetheart, there aren't services like that out here. You'd be lucky to get a package from the post office on time. That's small-town living and how it's always been."

"Yep. It's official. I actually *hate* it here," I tell him with my whole chest. "Can't wait to leave."

When his kettle whistles, he opens a package of hot cocoa and mixes it in a mug. "I plan to make some calls to see if there is any lodging in town for you."

"Great."

"But..."

The way he lingers is unsettling.

"Don't get your hopes up. It's the holiday tourist season, and a lot of skiers are waiting to hit the slopes after the blizzard. Plus, with Christmas coming up, people come in for the festival and to visit their families. It'd be a miracle to find something right now."

Considering what Peggy told me, I know he's telling the truth. *Just lovely.*

Just as I open my mouth, our phones blare with an alert that nearly has me jumping out of my skin.

"Looks like all the roads in and out of here are closed," he says as I read the message from the National Weather Association about dangerous winds, snow, and ice.

"Of course they are," I mutter dryly. "Do you have Wi-Fi?" I ask when a notification pops up to connect.

"Yeah, the password is Jolly1225 with a capital J. No spaces."

"You're joking." I raise a brow, and he shakes his head. I glance at the Christmas tree, the town scene on his mantel, and then back at him. "Is there a reason it looks like Christmas threw up in your house? I lost count of how many decorated trees and ridiculous amounts of décor you have everywhere."

He arches a brow.

"Wait. Do you have kids or something?" I blurt out.

This makes him chuckle. "No. But maybe one day."

"A girlfriend or wife going to barge in on us and think something's going on?" I ask just in case. There's no way he did all this for himself. It'd take months.

He shakes his head. "Nope. It's just Dasher and me."

"Oh." Not sure if that makes me feel better or worse.

"Did you touch my reindeer?" he asks.

"Huh?"

He points at the mantel. "I noticed he had been moved."

"I was looking around and wanted to see its face. I was in disbelief that someone actually lives like this."

He shakes his head. "I should've known something was off when I saw that."

"You're telling me. You missed my coat hanging on the rack, my boots by the door, and not to mention my whole-ass minivan in the driveway, but you noticed a small figurine not in the right spot?"

"I came in through the back door. Never saw your car or items. Besides, I like Christmas." He shrugs unapologetically.

"You're a little too old to be nerding out for Santa," I tell him, finding it quite refreshing, but I'd never admit that to him.

"Never too old for holiday spirit." He winks and makes his way into the kitchen.

"You hungry?" He flashes a boyish grin, showing off his perfect white teeth.

"Actually, I am."

He places a cast iron pan on the stove and turns on the burner. Then he pulls bacon and eggs from the fridge. Not that I'm purposely gawking, but it's hard not to as this lumberjack of a man cooks for me.

He glances over his shoulder at me as I try to understand his schtick. "So…is this Christmas thing a part of your identity or something? Do you work for Santa?"

He chuckles with amusement. "Do you hate the holidays?"

"I guess you could say that."

"You're joking," he deadpans like I'm the psychopath here when he has mistletoe hanging in his doorway with no one to kiss.

"No. I don't celebrate it at all."

And his smile I'm admittedly getting used to fades.

"You do realize that you are visiting the place that's fabled to have been the original North Pole?"

"Please." I roll my eyes as I sit at the breakfast bar and wait. "I'm aware, and from what I saw when I drove through, I'm not that impressed. I've seen more believable movie sets built in California parking lots."

"Now that's just offensive. Just wait until you witness it in its full glory during the winter festival," he tells me while fixing our plates.

Guilt nearly slaps me in the face because it's not my intention to shit all over his town. However, the last thing I need is a new friend who's holiday obsessed when I'm actively trying to avoid it.

"Levi." I grab his attention as he sets our plates down on the breakfast bar. "I want to apologize for how I reacted last night and for macing you. Not that it's an excuse, but I had a horrible day getting here, and had to drive over two hours in this weather."

"You drove that far?"

"Yeah, my flight got canceled, and I didn't want to wait in the airport overnight."

"Wow, that sucks. I'm shocked you made it here in one piece."

"Me too," I say honestly. "But anyway, who leaves their door unlocked?"

"I was outside chopping wood," he explains. "Didn't realize I had to dead bolt it to stop Goldilocks from getting comfy in my bed."

His smirk has me glaring at him. "Very funny. You act like I purposely snuck in."

"I'm not the only one to blame here, babe. You didn't see how lived in the house was and think maybe you were in the wrong place?"

Before I can argue, the lights flicker. I pick up my phone, and Levi does the same.

"We just lost Wi-Fi. The router will restart, but there might be an area-wide outage," he tells me.

I try to text my sister, but it shows *not delivered*. "My text won't go through."

Levi looks at his screen. "We just lost cell service. A tower might've went out. That sometimes happens with high winds."

"Shit," I mutter, realizing I'm in a worse position than I was when I arrived. Not only don't I know this man but now I have no way of calling or texting anyone for help if he turns out to be a total psycho. While he seems like a genuinely nice guy, some people are great at faking it. And considering what his house looks like, I wouldn't put him being a psycho off the table just yet.

"Well, there's nothing we can do, just gotta make the best of it," he tells me as his dog lies at my feet. I look down and meet his big brown eyes, then throw him a piece of bacon when Levi isn't looking. Dasher wags his tail as I sneak him another.

"Don't worry about yesterday. Everyone deserves a second chance, but what matters is what you do with it."

"Philosophical, too," I hum. "As soon as I find somewhere else to go, I'll be out of your hair. I have a lot of work to do and need zero distractions. I don't like being interrupted when I'm in the zone."

"Are you setting ground rules?" he teases. "Either way, I won't bother you."

"I have to get this article just right."

"Article or *exposé* piece?" he challenges.

"What's that supposed to mean?" I retort.

"You said you already hate it here. Just wondering if you came with good or bad intentions. An article written in a bad light could ruin our town's businesses and tourist attractions."

"Are you trying to intimidate me to write a puff piece?"

He grins slyly. "I don't think anyone could intimidate you. Especially with you carrying around deadly weapons."

I roll my eyes at his dramatics. "As of now, my only priority is to be truthful. I want to visit the local farms and meet the people who run them, as well as interview the mayor, business owners, and tourists. I've done some research and read a few blogs. As of now, I don't believe it's all it's cracked up to be."

"I can't believe they sent a Christmas-hating journalist to one of the jolliest places on the planet who also happens to have the last name of Joy. Do you find the humor in that at all? Or is your heart really made of coal?" He laughs, taking a bite of eggs.

"That's so funny coming from a guy with the last name of *White*... whose family owns a Christmas tree farm and is obsessed with reindeer and Santa."

He taps his temple. "It's called smart marketing, baby." He shoots me a wink, and I hate how heat rushes through my body when he looks at me like that.

I finish eating, then place my plate in the sink. "Thanks for breakfast."

"You're welcome. I'm making it my personal mission to get you to like this holiday before you leave. You'll be singing Christmas songs in no time."

"Don't get your hopes up. Christmas has been dead to me for years," I say without thinking as I make my way to the stairs.

"Wait, what?" he calls out, but I go to my room and ignore his question.

I wish I could call Taryn and tell her what's going on and how memories of our childhood flood my mind every time I stare at one of these trees. But since I can't do that, I open my laptop and pull up a blank document.

At least we still have electricity…*for now*.

First impressions are everything, and based on what's happened since I've arrived, this place seems more like a winter hell than a wonderland.

So I place my fingers on the keys and do what I fall back on anytime I get overwhelmed—I write.

CHAPTER FOUR

LEVI

GETTING STUCK during a blizzard with a complete stranger who maced me while I was buck-ass naked was the last thing on my Bingo card.

But here I am, isolated with Little Miss Seattle and her Christmas-hating attitude.

There's no telling how long cell service will be out. My best guess is at least until the wind dies down. The last time a storm this big came through, I didn't have reception for a week.

I pray that isn't the case this time.

Only a few hours have passed, and Fallon's already driving me crazy because she *needs* to get ahold of her assistant or boss or whoever-the-fuck knows. The girl couldn't live off the grid if her life depended on it.

After we eat lunch in awkward silence, I go outside and make sure the generator is ready in the event we lose power. The lights have been flickering, so I have no doubt it'll happen.

The cold doesn't bother me, but given that Fallon's already wearing two layers, I assume she's not a fan.

After I look everything over, I contemplate hopping on my snowmobile to check on my parents. The snow continues to fall heavily, and I can't risk getting stuck at my folks' and leaving Fallon here alone. Only God knows what would happen to her, and I can't bear that responsibility.

Plus, my mom and dad have been through countless blizzards, so I know they're fine.

When I walk inside carrying as much wood as I can, Fallon's pacing the living room like reception will magically appear. I stack the logs neatly by the fireplace, wondering if I should make another trip outside.

"This is unreal," Fallon mutters, tossing her phone on the sofa with a huff. Her laptop is open on the coffee table, and she curses under her breath. "How am I supposed to charge my laptop if we lose power?"

"What will you need it for if there's no internet?" I ask.

With a hand on her hip, she twists and glares at me. "I can still write, but I won't be able to make much progress if the battery dies."

I scrub a hand through my hair, biting my tongue by how worked up she is. "If the electricity goes out, the generator will automatically kick on to run the fridge, a couple of lights, and the water well pump. One plug is connected but should only be used on an emergency basis. If it's overloaded, we could overheat or destroy the generator completely. That'd leave us in complete darkness and without food. However, if you need to charge your computer for an hour, that should be fine."

She rolls her eyes as if I'm responsible for this inconvenience.

"On the bright side, I have propane, so we can still use the stove and take hot showers."

"*Great,*" she says with fake enthusiasm. "I didn't know people actually lived like this."

"Like what?" I kneel to pet Dasher and try not to sound offended.

"Off the grid..." She waves a hand through the air. "In the wilderness...the middle of nowhere. Sounds dangerous if you ask me. What if there's an emergency?"

I chuckle because her idea of being *off the grid* is comical. "I'm twenty minutes from town. I'd hardly call that roughing it."

"You don't even have cable. Or food delivery."

"No, but I have working appliances and a pantry full of food. Plus, I can stream shows and movies, which works decently enough on my Wi-Fi...well, except in this weather."

"Of course." She sighs, her hands smacking her knees when she finally takes a seat and gives my rug a break.

"I'm gonna grab some more logs while I can and let Dasher run around. Wanna join me?" I ask politely.

She frowns with a side-eye that confirms she will *not* be going outside.

As soon as I open the door, Dasher flies off the deck and into a huge snow bank. He still has as much energy as he did the day I brought him home two years ago. If it were up to him, he'd live outside twenty-four seven.

"C'mon, Dash. This way." I head toward the wood shed. I'm used to being out here alone. I like it and don't mind the quiet. It's peaceful, and the views are irreplaceable. Having Fallon here for the past couple of days has been an interesting change and a reminder of what it's like to have someone around. Too bad she's a grinch who wouldn't know happiness if it plowed into her.

Also, who the hell hates Christmas?

A beautiful woman who's snippy as fuck, that's who.

I can't help but wonder if her biases will find their way into her writing. She could have a huge impact, and not in a good way. It's already hard enough for local small businesses to keep up, and a bad feature could negatively affect their revenue. The holiday tourists shop a lot, and that money keeps them afloat throughout the year.

I was born and raised here and won't let some grumpy spoiled city girl tear it down.

If I could talk to my best friend, Finn, he'd tell me to do whatever it takes to make sure that doesn't happen. Show her what the town is really about—community, holiday spirit, and a place people visit to reconnect.

As soon as this storm passes, I'll give her a personal tour and show her everything we have to offer. It's a shame she's so reluctant because the town goes all out to create a magical holiday experience for visitors. Even if her first impressions haven't been great, I'll personally make sure she enjoys herself the rest of the time she's here.

As soon as the wheelbarrow is full, I whistle, and Dasher comes running behind me, beating me to the house. I roll and set the load down on the deck and then open the door.

"Hey, Fallon!" I call out and wait for her to approach. "Hold out your arms."

She raises her brows. "For what?"

"You stay here, you work here. Carry these logs inside."

I scoop them up and wait for her to comply. "You want extra heat or not?"

She sighs, finally agreeing. Carefully, I set a small stack of wood in her arms, and my hand runs along her wrist, repositioning a few so they don't fall loose.

"Got 'em?"

"Yeah. Now what?" She glares, which is unfortunate. She's too pretty to always be scowling. Her long dark-brown hair is silky smooth, and images of yanking it hard as I take her from behind run through my mind. Just thinking about widening her thick thighs as her green eyes pierce through me has me growing hard.

"Set them next to the fireplace, then come back for more," I say, adjusting myself when she turns around.

Dasher follows her into the house, and I hear her scold him for stepping on her heels. I snicker at how eager Dasher is for her affection.

After the fourth load, Fallon stomps back to me and huffs. "How much more? My arms are tired."

I hand her one more pile and wait as she secures them. "Last one for now. I'm gonna go grab more."

"Since I unloaded this one alone, you can do that one, then."

I arch a brow in amusement. "If we're playing by those rules, then you can cook dinner since I made lunch."

"Alright, but don't blame me if you get food poisoning."

"Oh, c'mon. You can't be that bad."

"I once set my oven on fire making a cauliflower pizza," she deadpans. "So yeah, don't trust me in the kitchen because I'm never home in time to eat dinner."

"Wait...how'd you manage that? Also, cauliflower on anything sounds disgusting."

She looks too embarrassed to answer and spins around, marching toward the fireplace. Instead of letting her get away, I follow her.

"You left the cardboard on, didn't you?"

"Maybe." She walks in a maze around Dasher as he relentlessly tries to get her attention.

"What'd you have the oven set to? Five hundred?" I taunt.

She drops the logs beside the others, then brushes the loose bark off her sweater. "If I tell you, no laughing."

I withhold a smirk and cross my arms. "No promises."

She scoffs. "You're...not wrong. I was reading something on my phone while setting the temperature, and I guess I didn't realize what I'd done until it was *way* too late."

Scratching a hand over my beard, I hold back laughter as I grin. "Yep, that'll do it. So no pizzas, then. Doesn't mean you're completely helpless."

"Gee, thanks."

"Anyone can learn the basics if they try."

"I can manage a bowl of Honey Nut Cheerios."

I pat my stomach. "I do love me some cereal."

She snorts, and I swear a faint smile touches her lips, but it quickly vanishes. "Fine, I'll help as long as you don't make me cook."

"Deal."

We go through the process again. Dasher closely follows her every move, and she curses when she trips over him during the final load.

"You okay?" Luckily, I catch her before she does a face-plant on the floor.

"No, I'm not." She blows out a frustrated huff, and I quickly release her. "I don't have coffee, internet, or any type of delivery services. When I'm pissed or annoyed, I usually go for a run, and now I can't even do that!"

"*Fallon...*" I say carefully, hoping to pull her off the ledge.

"For all I know, you're a murderer and put up the *fake listing* to get me here. It's probably why you live out in the middle of fucking nowhere! Trap your victims in your big secluded mountain cabin and then slaughter them."

"Mm-hmm...and I suppose I'm to blame for this blizzard too, right? I mean, I must've planned that. Summoned the angels above to bring us over twenty inches of snow and hurricane-force winds. I had to make sure you had no possible way to call for help or have access to your precious outside world. Damn, you caught me."

"Don't deflect with a smart-ass attitude. I watch enough true crime to know how serial killers premeditate their kills."

I chuckle, entertained by her theory. "If that were my plan, wouldn't I have killed you already instead of given you a place to sleep?"

"Some psychos enjoy playing with their prey first. Get me to trust you, and then that's when you make your lethal move." She makes a throat-slit motion, and I crack up.

"No wonder you're a writer. You have quite the imagination."

"But you're not denying it." She arches a brow, and I can't believe how serious she is.

Leaning in, I dip down to her ear and whisper, "Keep talking shit, and I'll put a pearl necklace around your throat instead."

"Uh...*what*?" She looks thoroughly confused until it finally hits her, and her eyes widen in shock.

I flash her a wink as the blood drains from her face.

Fuck, she's too damn easy to mess with, and although it's fun to rile her up, I have to finish gathering supplies right now.

"I'm gonna grab the extra lanterns, flashlights, and batteries. I have a kerosene lamp, too, just in case we're without power for a while."

She stays glued to the couch with Dasher next to her. I quickly build a fire since the house has a chill from the door being open, then search for everything we'll need.

When I return, she silently watches me like she's concerned I'll really gut her like a fish.

"Hungry?" I ask.

"Sure." Fallon sounds less than enthusiastic. While I'm sympathetic because she's not used to this, she better suck it up. This storm is just getting started.

A loud pounding startles me awake, and I roll over in bed to check the time on my phone. I went to sleep a few hours ago after Fallon and I ate dinner.

I whip open the door, and Dasher rushes toward Fallon. From what I can see, she's wrapped in a blanket.

"What's wrong?" I ask, hearing her teeth chatter.

"The heat's out, and I'm turning into an ice cube."

"I put extra blankets in your room," I explain, feeling the chill in the air. "The furnace should still be working even with the power out."

"Well, it's *not*," she whines. "And the blankets aren't enough when it's negative thirty outside."

"One was *wool*," I tell her in disbelief. She's being dramatic.

"Hey, I can't help it if I'm always cold."

"Because you're cold-hearted?"

"Can you save the insults for later, please? I'm having a crisis at the moment."

I smirk, grabbing her hand so she doesn't trip down the stairs. "C'mon, I'll build a fire."

Dasher zooms to the living room, and I grab a couple of flashlights and the matches.

"Hold this up for me so I can see." I hand her a flashlight.

I grab some kindling, but because of the draft, it takes me a minute to get it started. Once I have a nice flame going, I stand. "Is that better, Little Miss Seattle?"

She sits directly in front of the fire on the shag rug. Dasher settles in beside her, much to her disdain.

"Can you get him off me, please?" She tries to push against him, but he's a hundred-plus pounds of dead weight and doesn't budge.

"It's a mystery to me why he likes you so much. At least you can use his warmth." I grin.

She groans.

I can hear the fridge running. "Generator kicked on, so at least the food in the fridge won't go bad."

"And heat?"

"The pilot light must've blown out. Sometimes that happens when it's this windy. I'll check it in the morning when it's daylight."

She shoots me a disapproving glare. "So now what?"

"I'm going to bed. You should go back to sleep."

"Where? It's an icebox in my room."

I point at the couch.

"You're *kidding*."

Shrugging, I call for Dasher, who gives Fallon's cheek a final lick before following me out of the living room.

"The wooden bench by the window contains more blankets. Help yourself," I call out, and as I make my way upstairs, I swear I hear her cursing me. But I expect nothing less, considering her attitude.

CHAPTER FIVE

FALLON

DAY 3

I'M IN HELL.

No, scratch that.

It's too cold to be hell.

More like if hell was in Antarctica, and it was hailing and snowing ten-inch icicles.

Dramatic? Maybe.

But I *hate* it and loathe being cold even more.

My apartment is set to seventy-five nearly year-round, and although Seattle doesn't get super hot, it also doesn't get super cold. It rains half the time, which means I'm often wearing layers anyway.

This weather, though?

My worst fucking nightmare.

Waking up on Levi's couch, barely able to feel my fingers—even though I'm wearing gloves—has me groaning. Flashbacks of last night have me grinding my teeth with frustration. Levi suspects the furnace's pilot light blew out, and with how my luck's going, who knows if he can fix it.

The fireplace is down to its last log, so I begrudgingly stalk over and throw two more inside. As soon as I do, ash blows in my face, and I cough.

Of fucking course.

I wipe my eyes and cheeks, then wrap a blanket around me before going to the bathroom.

Once I'm done, I stare at my reflection in the mirror and wince. I need a hot shower, an avocado breakfast bowl, and a gallon of coffee.

I splash water on my face and brush my teeth. A rush of cool air seeps in through the vent, and I shiver. Last night, the wind howled against the windows, and I felt like I was sleeping outside. No way can I stay upstairs if there's a repeat of that. Although the couch wasn't uncomfortable, being cold and in a new place made it hard to fall into a deep sleep. Every little sound woke me, and I constantly had to remind myself where I was.

Once I rewrap myself in the blanket, I go downstairs but stop when I notice Dasher took my spot on the couch.

"Where the hell did you come from?" I walk closer and point at the floor. "Off."

He stares at me as if he's already bored with this conversation.

"Dasher. Off the couch. Now," I say in a deeper voice to mimic Levi's. He doesn't move.

"C'mon, let's go..." I pull on his collar to show him what I want, but he still doesn't budge.

"Dasher, I'm serious. I was lying there. You can sit on the rug." I reach for his collar again, but he licks my hand instead.

I sigh with exhaustion because I just wanted one more hour of sleep now that it's finally comfortable in here.

"Go." I wave my hand. "Outside? Want a treat? How about a nice long walk?" I ramble off as many trigger words as I can think of, but he's cemented in place.

"I think you're more stubborn than me," I mutter, crossing my arms.

"Doubtful," Levi says, chuckling.

"Jesus Christ." I jump, clenching a hand to my chest.

"Good morning," he singsongs.

"Trust me, it's not."

The corner of his lips tilts up, and it's then I realize he's shirtless and only wearing black boxer briefs. Is that what he had on last night?

How the hell is he not freezing his nuts off right now?

"A little help here?" I point at Dasher. "He won't listen."

Levi snaps his fingers. "Dasher, down."

He immediately obeys and wags his tail as he follows Levi to the kitchen.

"Seriously?" I throw out my arms, then ask, "Hey, any chance we'll get some heat today?"

"I'll check the pilot light after breakfast, but with the way the wind is blowing, I wouldn't get your hopes up."

"Of course," I murmur, sitting on the sofa and turning toward Levi.

I watch as he strolls around the kitchen, fills up a kettle, and sets it on the stovetop. Then he refills Dasher's water and opens a can of dog food.

"Come sit up here. I'll make you a cup of apple cider. It'll warm you up."

Reluctantly, I do as he says and end up staring at his body while he prepares it. Hard muscles line his back all the way below his shorts and down his legs. I can tell he's an active, outdoorsy type of guy just by his build.

I blink as he spins around and places a steaming hot mug on the breakfast bar. With a wide smile, Levi pops in a cinnamon stick.

"It tastes like Christmas in a cup!" He holds up a finger as I reach for it. "Blow on it first."

Levi happily studies me with anticipation for my approval.

"Are you always this bubbly in the morning?" I ask before taking a sip.

"Yeah, pretty much. What's not to love about this time of year?" He shrugs, and I want to respond with *every-fucking-thing*, but I don't. "Families shopping together, picking out and decorating their Christmas tree, baking cookies and making gingerbread houses, sleigh rides, the festive music. I enjoy the whole vibe of togetherness and giving. It's the *best* time of the year."

Oh God, he can't be serious.

This is my own personal hell.

He sounds like an eight-year-old boy excited to sit on Santa's lap instead of a thirtysomething man.

"Just wait until you experience the town in all its holiday glory. We're famous for our downtown festivals, small locally owned shops, and of course, Bennett's Orchard Farm. My best friend, Finn, and his family run it. I'll show you around so you can write a genuine, *honest* review for your article."

I stare at him like he's grown a second head. What makes him think any of that sounds appealing to me?

"Can't wait," I deadpan, lifting the mug to my lips and trying it.

"What do you think?" he asks enthusiastically.

"It's...not awful."

But it most definitely isn't coffee.

He frowns. "Stir it with the cinnamon stick. You'll thank me later." Then he shoots me a wink and starts digging in the fridge.

I do as he suggests and take a few more sips for the simple fact that it's warming my core.

Dasher sits next to Levi as he scrambles eggs, sausage, and cheese in a bowl before dumping it into the hot pan. Considering I'm starving and should be grateful for the food, I decide to keep my mouth shut about how I don't eat pork.

After hardly eating anything yesterday, I'll take what I can get, even this cinnamon sugar-water he claims is the best thing ever.

"Bon appétit!" Levi sets a plate in front of me, and while it looks decent, the smell of the meat makes me want to vomit.

"Thank you."

"Want a refresher?" He nods to my half-empty mug.

"No, I'm good."

I dig in, separating the sausage from the eggs and cheese. As we sit in silence, I slyly lower my hand and give Dasher the meat without Levi noticing. I glance down at him, and we make an unspoken agreement—I feed him, and he doesn't tell. Our little secret.

When my plate's empty and I've drained my mug, Levi grabs my dishes and stands.

"Um, thanks," I say, not used to anyone picking up after me. "I can take care of that." I quickly stand and walk toward the sink.

"You sure you know how?" He shoots me a smirk, and I roll my eyes. "Just figured that if you can't cook..."

"Rude." I scowl, and he chuckles.

"And just for that, I withdraw my offer." I return to the couch, dragging my blanket with me. To my displeasure, Dasher follows.

I curl up into a ball, basking in the warmth of the fire. When Levi comes into view, he's wearing gray sweatpants.

Tightly corded muscles line his stomach and arms, making me swallow hard as I avoid his gaze. He most definitely caught me gawking.

Shit. He needs to put on more clothes.

"I'm gonna check the furnace and see if I can get the pilot light to stay on."

I almost offer to help, but I know he'd probably make a joke about my lack of skills, so I sink back into the couch instead.

"Alright, I better add more layers in the event you fail," I mock. I'm already wearing two pairs of fuzzy socks, a long-sleeve shirt underneath a heavy sweatshirt, and two layers of leggings. No matter what I do, I can't get the chill out of my veins.

"Pretty mouthy for someone who'd never be able to survive living off the grid."

"That's not true," I argue, though it is. "I just choose not to put myself through that torture."

He licks his lips, pulling them back into a cocky grin as he scrubs his hand over his scruffy chin. "Okay, Little Miss Seattle. You're getting a lesson in country living. Come on."

He walks away before I can ask any questions, but I follow him anyway. When he opens the door to a utility room, I know I'm in trouble.

"Hold this for me." He hands me a flashlight without waiting for me to respond. Apparently, I'm his permanent flashlight holder. "Now aim it down here for me."

I kneel and do as he says, sneezing when he brushes off a layer of dust.

"You allergic?" he asks, crouching next to me.

"To filth? Yes."

He snorts.

"Just hold it steady."

After ten minutes of the pilot light coming on and flickering off, he shrugs his shoulders in defeat.

"It's not gonna stay lit."

"What's wrong with it?" I rush out, my breath floating in the crisp air in white bursts.

"Either it's still too windy or a sensor went bad and needs to be replaced."

"Is that easy to fix?" I ask.

"For a professional, yeah, but it's not something I'm equipped to do."

We both stand. "Really? I thought the Christmas-mountain man-lumberjack could fix and do anything."

He smirks as if he's amused. "Within my skill set, sure. But I'm not an electrician and don't have spare parts lying around to replace something like that."

I sigh with an eye-roll. *Just great.*

He waves out his hand. "But hey, if you wanna give it a shot and tinker around until your ass gets zapped, be my guest. Just remember, I can't get you to a hospital."

I toss the flashlight at him, and he shoots me a shit-eating smirk. "I'll take that as a no."

He crosses his arms, and I still can't believe he's shirtless and not getting frostbite.

"Just so you know, I'm rating your *listing* a zero out of five. Bad weather, no heat or power, clingy dog, and overly happy owner who walks around half naked. *Do not recommend*," I deadpan.

He throws his head back with a laugh. "It's not *my* listing. Surely, we've been over that."

I teasingly narrow my eyes at him and place a hand on my hip. "Yeah, I'm still not convinced this wasn't a part of your plan. Do you dump the bodies in the pond?"

Levi inches closer, catching me off guard. One side of his lips turns up in a mischievous grin as he lowers his mouth to my ear. "Sweetheart, if that was the case, your relentless complaining would've ensured you didn't make it past the first twelve hours. But instead, I fed you and made sure you were warm. Not to mention, the pond's frozen. It'd be a helluva lot easier to burn your body. No one would even bat an eye at a winter bonfire."

His deep, hoarse voice sends a shiver down my spine as his breath floats over my ear like a secret.

"That's actually incredibly disturbing. By the depth of your description, it sounds like you really want to convince me that this was a scam," I shoot back, but I'm not as confident as I sound.

A sparkle in his eyes flashes with amusement before he winks. "Guess you'll find out soon enough."

I swallow hard, though I know he's *probably* harmless. No serial killer could be more jolly than Santa Claus himself.

"That's not funny."

Grinning, he tenderly grabs my shoulder. "You're shivering. Let's get you back in front of the fire."

I don't tell him my body is actually on fire, and *he's* the reason for it.

Once the goose bumps leave my arms, I head up to my room. Even though there's no connection to the outside world, I need to start writing about my first impressions of this so-called famous holiday town.

After I've added another layer of socks and a third sweater, I slide under the covers and open my laptop. Luckily, I charged it before the power went out, so I have a full battery.

I type my intro paragraph about my experience thus far, which hasn't been good, but then I write myself notes to include later when I finally go into town.

When my door swings open, Dasher struts in and quickly jumps on my bed. He circles a few times before settling next to my legs.

"Dasher, down," I demand, snapping my fingers.

Instead of following directions, he rolls onto his back and waits for me to rub him.

"You're pitiful," I murmur, giving in and scratching his belly. Maybe then he'll leave and give me space.

Soon, Dasher's leg shakes as I find the perfect spot to itch. "There, we good?"

Levi's cackling causes me to jump, and I find him leaning against the doorframe with his arms folded. His goofy smile has my heart beating in overdrive, which is stupid.

This man and his dog drive me crazy.

"Dasher must be winning you over," he says.

"Not likely. He wouldn't listen to my commands, so I thought if I gave him what he wanted, he'd go away."

"Take it as a compliment," he states. "Dasher's a good judge of character." Then he shrugs with a smirk. "Or at least I *thought* he was."

"Ha ha," I say dryly. "He's the one who acts like he's never seen a female before. Guess you don't get many visitors in your bed, huh?"

He clenches a fist to his heart. "Damn. That one hurt."

I snort, though I try to hide my smile. There's no way this six-foot mountain of a man doesn't get laid every damn weekend.

"I'm going to take Dasher outside to run around, then take a shower. While I'm gone, think of what you might want for lunch this afternoon so I don't keep the fridge open too long. It's not running at its normal temp."

"Quinoa burrito bowl with fresno queso and an espresso would be wonderful, thank you."

"Hmm...the best I can do is chili with sliced cheese and instant coffee."

I make a face of disgust. "There goes your five-star rating."

"That's not what most of my female guests say. What can I improve?"

The way my heart lodges in my throat is unexplainable, but I ignore it and continue staring at Levi's perfectly shaped lips.

"Boundaries, for starters. If I'm not walking around half naked, then neither should you. And keep your dog out of my room."

I sound harsher than I mean to, but his amused expression has me wanting to knee him between the legs. Nothing I say seems to get under his skin, and that pisses me off.

His smirk tells me everything I just said has already rolled off his shoulders. "Duly noted. C'mon, Dasher. She doesn't like us. Outside."

I watch as the furball follows Levi out the door, neither looking back at me. There's no way I can get back to writing now, not with the images of him clouding my mind.

A few more minutes pass, and I actually feel a tad guilty for snapping. I let out a long sigh and lean back on my pillow. Levi's trying to scale the wall of my heart, but I can't let him. I am anti-charming men just as much as I'm anti-all things Christmas. He just happens to be the deadly combination of both.

CHAPTER SIX

LEVI

"READY, SET...GO!" I throw a tennis ball as far as I can for Dasher.

He runs at full speed toward the pond.

The snowfall has finally stopped, but the wind still feels like sharp blades cutting against my skin. However, Dasher loves it outside and still needs his exercise.

Plus, it gives me a moment away from Fallon's delicious death glare and gorgeous face. And those lips that I so desperately want to see form a smile, preferably around my cock.

Every time I'm around her, I prepare for a verbal punch in the gut, and she hasn't disappointed me yet.

Whatever her problem is, I'm determined to find out why this holiday puts her in such a sour mood. Still, her pouting and dislike for it amuse the hell out of me. She's trying so hard to be upset, which I know isn't an ideal situation for either of us, but she's succeeded at taking it to the next level. The difference is I'm making the best out of it while I can.

Before I stepped outside, I got fully dressed and put on my winter boots. Now that I've been running around with Dasher and throwing his ball, I'm sweating.

When I finally coax Dasher to come inside, I refill his water bowl, then head upstairs to shower.

As soon as I walk into the bathroom and see Fallon soaking in my tub, I come to a stop.

"Enjoying yourself?"

Her eyes blink open as she sinks deeper under the suds. But I already saw the tops of her breasts before I spoke.

"I thought you'd be outside for longer. Just wanted to relax and warm up."

"That costs extra. Should I add it to your tab?"

She groans with an eye-roll. "Very funny."

I shrug, yanking my shirt over my head and kicking off my boots. Then I unbutton my jeans.

"What are you doing?" Her voice wavers as her gaze lowers down my body.

"I came to take a shower. Dasher made me chase him around the yard before he'd come to the door."

"You can't wait until I'm done?"

"It's my house. Don't look if you're shy."

"I'm not..." She stops herself as I lower my pants, then my boxers.

I glance over as I turn on the water and catch her staring. She quickly averts her eyes, but I see the way she's looking.

For someone dead set on being miserable, she's not as good at acting as she thinks. I've had my fair share of women in my thirty-five years and can typically read them quite well.

Figuring out Fallon has become a fun new challenge.

"Can you at least turn around so *I* can get out, then?" she asks, draining the tub.

"Trust me, sweetheart. Nothing I haven't seen before."

She scoffs as I focus on her every step. Once she wraps a towel around her, she eagerly walks out, slamming the bathroom door behind her. Chuckling to myself, I lather soap over my body, then rinse off.

Fallon opts to skip lunch by ignoring me when I knock on her door, so she's starving by the time it's dark out.

She looks pitiful in her triple layers of clothes even though the roaring fire has heated the entire floor. So much that I'm sweating in athletic shorts and a T-shirt.

"Do you eat chicken?" I call out from the kitchen while she sits on the couch. She found a few books in my office and has been reading next to the kerosene lamp for the past few hours.

Though, I assume out of pure boredom because they're all historical fiction. Fallon doesn't seem like the type to read anything that isn't about modern-day fashion or celebrity memoirs.

"Yes," she answers wearily.

"So you're not a vegetarian?" I ask.

"No."

"Interesting."

"Why's that?"

"You eat chicken but not pork," I reply, and her head whips around to face me.

"How'd you know that?"

"You're more transparent than you realize." I smirk. "And definitely not as sly as you think."

Fallon frowns, biting the inside of her cheek.

"Pork is poisonous to dogs," I tell her. "You could've killed him. Good thing I had meds to give him so he'd puke it up."

"What?" The color drains from her face as I move around the kitchen, holding back the urge to laugh. Fuck, she's cute when she's gullible.

She looks around for Dasher as if she's truly worried, and guilt floods me for making her panic.

"Fallon." My deep timbre grabs her attention. "I'm kidding."

"Goddamn you!" She stands and stomps over, throwing her fist against my shoulder. "That was *mean*."

I snicker at her attempt to hurt me. "I'm sorry. You make it too easy to rile you up."

She stands in front of me with her arms crossed, pouting as she narrows her eyes in anger.

"I think you like him more than you want to admit," I taunt.

"No," she quickly responds. "I don't want a dog's death on my hands. That can't be good karma."

"Why didn't you just tell me you don't eat pork? You don't have to sneak around, Fallon. You aren't going to hurt my feelings because of something I made. My ego isn't that fragile."

"I didn't want to seem ungrateful," she says timidly. "Plus, it's not like you asked if I even wanted an omelet, so I just accepted what you made."

"Fair enough. But from now on, just say something, okay?"

"Okay."

"Chicken fettuccini, do you like that?"

"I try to avoid pasta, but considering the circumstances, I'll eat some while I'm here."

"What in the world do you even eat in Seattle? Tofu?"

"For your information, I have a gluten allergy, which is why I limit my pasta intake. It's not because I deprive myself of carbs. You've seen my thighs. Do you really think I'm a health nut? I just have to watch out for gluten, or I'll feel uncomfortable and bloated."

At the mention of her luscious legs, I imagine kneeling between them and licking her pussy until she explodes all over my tongue. Her body confidence is as sexy as her curvy hips.

Quickly shaking away the thoughts of her sitting on my face, I nod. "You don't have to eat it if you don't want to."

"I'll have a little. It actually sounds pretty good," she replies, no longer shooting daggers at me.

"Okay, it'll be ready in a half hour. Think you can make it until then?" I smirk when her stomach growls.

"I hope so."

"You wanna help? I'll cook the chicken if you want to start on the sauce."

"Do you have a recipe for me to follow?" She looks truly concerned that she'll fuck it up.

I tap my temple. "All up here, babe. I'll walk you through it."

For the next thirty minutes, we work side by side. She mixes and stirs the ingredients in a pot while I cut and sauté the chicken.

As the sauce simmers, I guide her through boiling the pasta. While she does that, I grab some plates and make our drinks.

"My stomach is going to eat itself soon," she whines, inhaling the scent of our food.

I laugh, enjoying this side of her. She hasn't glared at me once since we started cooking.

Once the sauce is done, I add in the chicken and let it marinate for a few minutes before she makes a plate. As soon as Fallon makes it to the table, she digs in.

"This sauce is so good," she moans around a piece of chicken, and I have to adjust myself as I sit across from her.

"I'll be the judge of that," I tease since she technically made it.

"Don't be rude now," she quips.

"Me? Look who's talking. I'm the nicest guy you'll ever meet."

She snorts, devouring her food. "Like I haven't heard that one before."

"Yeah, but I'm not like other guys."

She snorts. "Oh really? Give me all of your exes' numbers, and I'll find out for sure."

I raise a brow. "Oh, we're having the exes talk already? Wow, you really do move fast."

"Why are you so surprised? We're already living together." She scoops a forkful of food and devours it like she hasn't eaten in days.

I bark out a laugh. This flirty banter is something I haven't seen from her, and my cock likes it—*a lot*.

Maybe the key is keeping her fed. Perhaps she's just been hangry this whole time.

One can dream.

"How many exes are there?" she blurts out.

"So we really *are* having this discussion?"

"Sure, why not? Unless there's been a lot, and you can't count that high?"

I scratch my cheek in amusement, shoveling more pasta into my mouth as I pick my next words carefully.

"I haven't really had...*relationships* per se. Not sure they can be considered an ex if it wasn't ever serious."

"*Oh*, I get it now."

I eye her curiously. "What?"

"You're a fuck boy."

Her bluntness has me smirking. "I'm too old to be considered a fuck boy. I date women to see if we're a good match, and none have worked out long-term."

"Fine, fuck *man*." She shrugs, taking a bite of chicken and moaning. "Serial dater who's too afraid to settle down or commit—like every other man in this world. I'm sure you had no problem sleeping with them first before deciding they weren't *the one*."

"Sounds like you have me all figured out."

"Don't tell me I've hurt your feelings?"

"Yep, I'm gonna cry myself to sleep tonight."

She rolls her eyes as I crack a smile.

"I doubt you've ever cried over a woman in your life."

Jesus Christ. Says the one who's currently giving me emotional whiplash.

"Do you want more water?" I ask.

She furrows her brow at my abrupt subject change.

"Or should we talk about your dating history now?" I taunt.

"Absolutely not."

"I can't imagine why you'd have relationship issues," I say dryly, earning me a scowl. "With you being so pleasant and sweet, it's a mystery to me."

"Are you done?"

Her resting bitch face has me fighting back a smile because she's a natural.

"Dessert?" I ask, grabbing my plate and bringing it to the sink.

"Depends. Does it come with your sarcasm and bad jokes? Because if so, I'll pass."

"Suit yourself. Thirty-eight women think my jokes are *fuck-worthy*."

Her eyes widen in horror as she nearly chokes on her pasta. "Total or...*this year*?"

Instead of answering her, I grab a fudge pop from the freezer, then shoot her a wink.

I'll let *Judge Judy* overthink that one for a bit.

Fallon clearly has some serious past relationship trauma that she's externalizing onto me for the simple fact that I have a dick. She acts like every guy is out to hurt her, and if that's the case, I'll tread lightly. I want her to feel comfortable enough to drop the act and, eventually, her guard. Her brick walls are tall and built to withstand a Category 5 hurricane.

I'd like her to trust me and know I only have good intentions.

And in order to do that, she'll need to open up.

After dinner, we go our separate ways. She curls up on the couch, and Dasher, the traitorous shit, stays down with her while I go upstairs. It's pitch-black in my room, but I know every inch of my house like the back of my hand. But since Fallon doesn't, I make sure to leave a flashlight on the coffee table so she can find her way to the bathroom.

I strip down to my boxers and slide under the covers, hoping the power and phone service come back on tomorrow.

Since the storm has fully passed, the state snow plows should be out to clear the roads for the lineman. As long as the wind stays calm, I'll be able to clear the driveway so we can get out of the house. I'm ready to go back to the farm and show my favorite Ebenezer Scrooge around town.

I fall asleep with thoughts of Fallon on my mind, but when I wake to her soft voice, my first thought is that *I'm dreaming*.

"Levi," she repeats my name, shaking my arm.

"What is it?" I murmur.

"The fire needs more wood, and there's none left in the house," she tells me.

"How's that possible?" I turn toward her with half-opened eyes.

"I don't know, it's been burning for three days straight? Can you grab some more?"

"It's the middle of the night, Fallon. I'll do it first thing in the morning."

"But I'm freezing my ass off now. What do you expect me to do until then?"

I roll over and pull back the covers. "Get in."

"What?"

"I'll give you my body heat so you won't freeze to death."

My eyes finally adjust to the dark, and I see she's wrapped tightly in her blanket.

"How are you only wearing shorts?"

"The cold doesn't bother me, Fallon. You climbing in or what?"

"I guess you leave me no choice," she mutters bitterly, and I stifle a laugh. There's the Fallon I know.

"You're welcome to take off your clothes, too."

"Oh my God, you fucking creeper." She whacks my chest.

"Jesus Christ, woman. Do you know *any* survival skills?"

"Huh?" She pulls the covers up and snuggles underneath.

"Skin-to-skin contact helps regulate temperature so you warm up faster than you do wearing clothes," I explain.

"Oh, well...no thanks. I'm good."

"Okay, but if your razor blade nipples cut me, I'm suing."

The back of her hand finds my chest again, and I snicker.

"You sure you want to sleep next to a fuck boy?" I tease, throwing her own words at her.

"You gonna cry if I say no?"

This time I bellow out a laugh.

"You wound me, *Fallon Joy*."

"Oh, please. By your extensive condom collection, I doubt a woman has ever hurt your feelings."

"You went through my drawers, did ya?" I ask with amusement.

"That was before when I was unpacking some of my things. There were so many, I figured it was a perk for the renters or something. Didn't realize it was all for one lumberjack of a person."

"Careful. You sound jealous."

She scoffs. "You *wish*. Now stay on your side, and I'll stay on mine."

"The whole bed is *my* side."

"Unless you want a knee to the dick, you'll stay over there."

I chuckle. "Good night, Little Miss Seattle."

CHAPTER SEVEN

FALLON

DAY 4

I WAKE up to an empty bed. I reach over to Levi's side, but it's cool to the touch. Although I threatened him not to get too close last night, I woke up with his body pressed against mine. However, my threats were empty, and I soaked in his warmth like summer sunshine. I shouldn't trust him and don't, thanks to my previous shitty relationship, but I do believe he means well.

I suck in a deep breath, stretch, and then get out of bed. After I use the bathroom, I go downstairs and notice Levi putting on his boots. I take a second to admire him but quickly avert my eyes when he notices me.

"Breakfast is waiting for ya. No pork," Levi says with a wink.

"Thanks," I say, then gasp when I realize the power is fully on. *Finally.* "Going somewhere?"

"It's plow day," he explains. "Gotta take care of the driveway, the private farm road, and the parking lots. It'll probably take me all day, so I wanted to get started early. How'd you sleep?"

"Okay, I guess. Didn't feel like I was lying in a freezing tundra, so no complaints."

"Happy to be of service." He licks his lips, and I roll my eyes.

"Be of service and bring in more wood for me."

"Already done. Oh, I'm leaving Dasher with you today."

"Oh, uh, *no*. I didn't sign up to dog sit," I argue, putting a hand on my hip.

"And I didn't sign up for an unannounced houseguest. Guess we're both shit out of luck." He grabs his jacket off the hook by the back door. "Don't worry, he'll let you know when he needs to go out. Dog food is in the pantry. I already fed him this morning, but you can give him another can at dinnertime. He can have as many treats as you think he deserves. I left my number on the fridge. Add it to your phone, then text me. If there is an emergency, call me immediately."

"Levi! *Please, no*. Dasher doesn't listen to anything I say. How am I supposed to watch him while I work?"

"You were the one worried about murderers. I'm leaving you a guard dog. He'll protect you while I'm gone."

I give him a look and cross my arms.

"You really should be thanking me right now." He smirks, zipping up his coat.

"Oh, please. He's a bigger chicken than I am. If someone broke in, I'd have to protect *him*." I roll my eyes.

Dasher follows him, and Levi stops to pet his head. "Don't listen to her, and be a good boy."

"You literally just told him not to listen to me!" I shout, but he continues walking out the door.

I glance down at Dasher, who's looking up at me. "What? You're screwed. I'm not entertaining you."

Turning around, I go to the kitchen and find a plate of eggs and hashbrowns that are still warm. While I eat, Dasher sits at my feet, begging for some. Instead, I eat every bite, rinse the plate, then nearly trip over Dasher on the way to the living room.

I sit on the couch, watching the flames lick the inside of the fireplace, and wish I had a mug of coffee.

Dasher stares me down, then trots to his pile of toys as I grab my laptop. The first thing I do is try to connect to the Wi-Fi, and I nearly cry when it works.

Dasher has a squeaky ball in his mouth and places his head on the edge of the couch. While I catch up on emails, I try to ignore him, but he nudges his cold nose against my hand.

"Go lie down." I position my body away from him so he moves into my line of sight. It's impossible to avoid those big brown puppy dog eyes. Eventually, I pull the ball from his mouth and throw it as hard as I can across the room.

Biggest mistake of my life.

He immediately returns it, his tail wagging in excitement. I toss it again, and this time, it bounces off the wall bolting in the opposite direction. The pads of his feet tap along the hardwood floor as he retrieves the ball and brings it back to me.

I type an email to my boss with my free hand and eventually finish, but it takes me twice as long. Then I open my document and read the last paragraph I wrote.

Dasher whines, and I hold him off for five minutes, but then my heart can't handle his whimpering any longer. So his relentless game of fetch begins again.

After every few words I write, I throw that damn ball as far as I can. He doesn't take the hint that I'm *over it.*

"*Please.* I really need to work," I tell him as if he can understand. We play until he runs to the back door. For a moment, I think I'll get a break, that is, until he paws at it. I huff, set down my laptop, then meet him.

"Let's come to an agreement first. You do your business, then come right back. Got it?"

I wait, almost expecting an answer, but he just stares forward in anticipation.

"Okay, fine," I say, twisting the knob and opening the door. The first thing Dasher does is jump into a pile of snow.

"Oh God," I groan, stepping onto the deck to watch him run around. "Hurry up so we can go back inside!"

The cold air wafts into the house, and I shiver, wishing I had grabbed my coat. A sweater and a thermal aren't enough.

"*Dasher!*"

He bunny hops around, the bright green ball still in his mouth as he has the time of his life. I shut the door, trying to warm up, but keep an eye on him through the window. I tap on the glass, and he pops his head up with his ears raised. "Come on, go potty!"

He goes back to tossing the ball in the air and playing by himself. I shake my head, annoyed that I'm left to watch this spoiled animal who has no consideration for my productivity.

"Fine," I mutter and return to my laptop in the living room. If he's smart enough to let me know when he wants out, he should be smart enough to let me know when he wants back in.

Sighing, I look back at the steadily blinking cursor on my screen. I read over the few sentences I wrote while distracted, not fully impressed with them, and decide to delete them.

Until I see more, I won't be able to continue writing, so I stop forcing it. Instead, I text my sister with an update.

FALLON

> We lost power during the storm, and it just came back on. Sorry for not calling you back, but I'm safe.

TARYN

> I was worried to death about you! What do you mean, WE?

FALLON

> Long story. Can I call you?

Immediately, my phone rings. I explain every single detail, and when I stop to finally take a breath, she speaks up.

"Wow," she says. "So you're staying in this stranger's house until you find another place? Is he hot?"

I snort.

"I'll take that as a *yes*."

I shrug, trying to seem indifferent. "Kinda. But it doesn't matter because he's obsessed with the holidays. His family owns a Christmas tree farm, and it's his whole personality—including every inch of his house. We're complete opposites. He makes fun of me for not being able to survive out in the wilderness like a psycho."

She chuckles, and I know she's probably thinking the same thing as him. "Who cares. Not like you'll be calling him Santa Claus while getting tangled up in the sheets. I mean, unless you're into that kinda thing. Call him *St. Dick* while he rams your sleigh."

"Taryn," I scold. "Gross."

Just as a thought comes to me, I hear barking outside. "Shit. I've gotta let the dog inside before he loses his shit or runs off."

"Wait, you're taking care of his dog?"

"Yeah, and not because I want to. He forced it on me while he snow plows the driveway and his family's farm. And don't you dare make a plowing joke," I warn.

She snickers. "You know me so well. But anyway, I'm glad you're okay. I was ready to send a search and rescue party out for you, but then I Googled the town and saw how bad it was. Figured you lost power."

"Yeah, it was actually pretty scary. The wind sounded evil, and I nearly froze to death. I'm kinda tired, though. Haven't been sleeping that great since I got here. The heat went out, and my room is an icebox."

"You know what'll warm you right up?"

"What's that?" I amuse her.

"Lots and lots of sex."

"Not. happening."

"Never say never, Fallon. Especially now that you're practically living with this sexy lumberjack."

"Hopefully not for long. He's supposed to be calling around for a hotel for me."

"And what if there are no vacancies?"

I blow out a breath because I've wondered the same thing. "I haven't figured that out yet."

"I wouldn't sweat it. Doesn't sound like he's actively trying to get rid of you if you're dog-sitting," she says. "But anyway, I bet you have a lot to work to catch up on, so I'll let you get back to it."

"Thanks. Love you. I'll let you know what happens."

"Sounds great. Love you too."

I end the call, then go open the door for Dasher. He rushes in, drops the ball, then shakes. Cold water splashes all over me, and that's when I realize just how soaked and filthy he is. Before I can stop him, he runs through the house, paw prints and droplets trailing him.

"Dasher!" I shout, panicking when he shakes again and jumps on the couch. "God. Now it smells like a wet dog in here."

Shaking my head, I go to the bathroom and grab a towel to clean up the mess and another to dry him.

"You're gonna get us both in trouble," I murmur, though I doubt he gives a shit.

Once the floor is clean, I throw the towel over his back and soak up as much water as I can. "You're a stinky boy."

He leans forward and tries to lick me, but I dodge him. "Eww, no. Keep that to yourself."

When I pet his head, I realize his fur is cold to the touch. I throw another log on the fire, then grab a blanket and cover him. He rests his head and kicks out his legs.

"You're spoiled as fuck," I say, and I think he knows it, too.

"Also, I'm not bathing you. Your owner can do that when he gets home," I tell him. "I'm sure you'll need to go out again before then."

I return to my small corner on the couch since Dasher hogs most of it, then I pick up my laptop. Maybe he'll take a nap and give me a few hours of peace and quiet.

An email from Peggy states that she canceled my company card, and the unknown charges were reversed. It's a small silver lining in this shitty situation.

My mind races knowing that time is ticking. I didn't expect to be snowed in for days and had planned specific things to do. My schedule is now off-kilter, and it's stressing me out. Thankfully, Levi's already volunteered to be my tour guide, so hopefully, I can get back on track.

However, that means spending more time with Levi White and his overenthusiastic Christmas self.

CHAPTER EIGHT

LEVI

It FEELS like it's negative fifty with the windchill, and the harsh winds burn my skin. As I plow my driveway, I call Finn to touch base and make sure they're okay.

Although I know he survived just fine with his girlfriend, Oakley. When he answers, I give an update on my current situation. He nearly dies of laughter, as does Oakley. Their teasing is exactly what I expected.

Once I clear my road, I make my way to the Christmas tree farm. The amount of snow that fell in such a short time slows me down. It's been years since we've seen a storm of this magnitude. Any time there's a blizzard, I'm responsible for clearing the roads, especially since my dad is getting older.

After I clear the parking lot, I grab my shovel from the back of the truck and work on the sidewalks. Once I'm done, I take a quick picture and send it to my mom, who replies with a thumbs-up emoji. Tomorrow, the place will be thriving again, like we weren't just hit with over twenty inches of snow.

LEVI

Heading to your house now.

MOM

Sounds great. Be careful.

LEVI

You know I always am.

Their long driveway has a few curves, so I take my time clearing the road. They built their house a significant distance from the main road so the heavy traffic from the farm wouldn't interrupt their regular flow of life.

When my childhood home comes into view, I smile. The picturesque two-story log cabin is surrounded by hills covered in blankets of white. Smoke billows from the chimney, and the tree lights twinkle through the front window. I should get Oakley to paint a canvas of this for my parents. She's a talented artist, and I know she'd nail it. I snap a quick picture, so I don't forget.

I park, then quickly shovel their sidewalk.

My mom cracks open the front door. "When you're done, come inside."

"Alrighty." I chuckle, seeing my hot breath in the air.

Thirty minutes later, I go inside. It's toasty so I shake off my coat, scarf, and gloves.

"Pumpkin pie?" Mom asks from the living room, wrapped in a blanket as she flips through a magazine. "Baked it a couple of hours ago."

"Don't mind if I do."

"It's on the counter."

When I enter the kitchen, Dad's sitting at the table drinking coffee and reading on his tablet.

"Anything mind-blowing in the news?" I ask.

"Nope. Nothing has changed." He meets my eyes. "Did you finish plowing already?"

"Yeah, and now I'm ready for summer."

He snorts. "And just think, the cold and snowy season has just begun."

"I don't usually mind it, but damn, that blizzard was a monster." I grab a knife from the drawer and cut myself a big piece.

"I'll take another." Dad smirks as if he's not supposed to have more, but I serve him one anyway. I plop mine on a plate, then grab the whipped cream from the fridge and add a healthy dollop on both.

"Wanna hear a crazy story?" I join him at the table as my mom comes in and starts a fresh pot of coffee. "Glad you're in here, Ma. I was just about to tell Dad about my current predicament."

"Everything okay?" she asks.

"Well, I found a strange woman in my house and, more specifically, in my bed the day of the blizzard."

Dad gives me a look.

"No, I didn't invite her," I clarify before he can ask.

"Who is she?" Mom asks.

"Fallon Joy. She's a journalist from Seattle who's been assigned to write about the town."

"That doesn't explain why she was at your place," Dad tells me.

"She claims she'd rented it online. But I found that out after she maced me."

"Oh no, poor thing. I bet she was scared half to death," my mom says.

"What about me? My eyes burned all night long."

My dad chuckles. "So where is she now?"

"She's there watching Dasher for me. I offered her the guest room since the roads were closed, and she had nowhere else to go. But now I have to try to find her a hotel or something."

"You know that's not going to happen this time of year," Mom says.

"Still going to try. But if there's no luck, I'll let her stay because I can tell how important this project is to her. She's very dedicated."

"That's lovely, dear!" The excitement in Mom's voice is unmatched.

I give her a pointed look. "Except for the fact she's a grinch and hates Christmas. Should've seen her trying to survive without power or heat. You'd think her whole world collapsed."

Mom chuckles.

"What happened to your furnace?" Dad asks.

I explain the problem and remind myself to call about it on the way home.

"She lost her mind when she learned we don't have any food delivery services."

Dad smirks as he takes a sip from his mug. "Well, not everyone's built for this kind of weather and lifestyle, son. She's probably used to city living."

"No kidding. I genuinely want her to have a good time, and I'm worried she already hates it here."

Mom shoos my negativity away. "Don't stress about it, sweetie. Once she participates in the fun activities we have to offer, she'll change her mind. Is she going to the festival?"

"I think it's the main reason she's visiting."

"Well, I know how passionate you are about the holiday, so you're the perfect person for the job. Just take her around and allow her to experience the most magical time of year with you. I'm sure she'll adore it."

"You say that, but you haven't met her. I'll do my best."

Dad laughs while standing to make a fresh mug of coffee.

"Well, maybe you could bring her over for dinner one night? We'd be happy to chat with her."

"Maybe. I think I'll need to warm her up to the idea of meeting my family first. No need to throw her to the vultures right away."

Mom laughs. "Pfft. She'd be singing '*Jingle Bells*' by the time she leaves here."

I nearly choke on my pie. "Highly doubtful. It's more than obvious she isn't having a good time."

"Give the girl a chance. She's been stuck with you for days," Mom says with a sly smile.

"I'm not sure if that's a dig or a compliment," I say around a mouthful.

"Me either," Mom tells me.

Once Dad and I finish eating, I carry our plates to the sink and quickly rinse them. "Does Lucy need her driveway cleared?"

"Nah. Bart took care of it already," Dad explains.

Bart works for the farm and lives on the south side of the property, so he's closer. "Great, then I can finally go home and shower." I grab my jacket and put on my gloves. Before I grab my scarf, I turn to my mom.

"Do you happen to have some ground coffee for Fallon?"

"Of course. You know we stock up on that around here," she singsongs, heading toward the pantry. "Do you need filters too?"

"Yep."

"A coffee pot?" Mom peeks her head from the doorway and meets my eyes.

"No. I have one tucked away somewhere. I'm sure it still works."

"If for some reason it doesn't, let me know because I have an extra."

"Thanks, Ma." I give her a kiss on the cheek as she hands over the bag of supplies. Fallon is going to be so excited.

Once in the truck, I make my way across the property to my house. I call Jasper, the owner of the only heating and cooling company around here.

When he answers, I fill him in on the problem with my pilot light.

"I'm pretty backed up at the moment, but I can put you on my waitlist. Might be a couple of days, though." He sounds just as tired as me.

"I figured as much. I have a fireplace, so I'm not freezing, but it's not enough to warm the whole house. Anyway, I appreciate your help."

"No problem. I'll come and take a look as soon as I can. Now, getting parts is a whole other issue."

"I know how it is," I offer before we say our goodbyes. Honestly, I should've remembered to get the furnace serviced months ago, but it slipped my mind once the season started. On the rest of the drive, I call every hotel in town. The inns and bed and breakfasts are also rented until after the new year. As I suspected, nothing is available.

When I finally arrive home, exhaustion takes over. I grab my things, then make my way inside. Dried paw prints are on the floor, and I follow them toward the living room.

Fallon's fingers fly across the keyboard, and she doesn't stop until she finishes her thought. Then she looks over her shoulder at me. I move toward the fire and warm my ice-cold hands. I'm proud of her for keeping it lit all day.

"Oh, you're ridiculous." I look at Dasher sprawled out on the couch and take steps toward him. When I pet his head, his tail wags under the blanket she wrapped him in. "Oh, you stink."

I turn to Fallon, who's dressed in tight joggers, at least two pairs of fuzzy socks, and a hoodie.

"How was your day?" I ask, knowing he probably wore her out.

"Horrible," she mutters, and I hand her the bag of goodies. She struggles to untie the handles that are in a tight bow.

"It couldn't have been *that* bad," I say. "At least not any worse than mine."

"Debatable." Her eyes widen once she opens the bag. "You brought me coffee? Oh my God."

Her mood immediately changes.

"Compliments from my mama," I offer.

"I'll have to personally thank her," she says genuinely, and I know my mom will like that.

"So tell me how my precious little boy was a demon." I smirk, knowing just how rambunctious he can be.

"First of all, he brought me that ball and forced me to throw it for nearly an hour."

My face cracks into a wide smile at her emphasis on *forced.*

"And then, when I let him out, he kept playing in the snow and slush. Every time I tried to get him to come in, he'd act like it was a game, but I absolutely was not chasing after him. I finally just left him out there until he pawed on the door to tell me he wanted in," she explains. "Also, I'm sorry he's gross. I made a valiant effort to clean up the paw prints but eventually gave up. It was useless."

Now, I'm laughing. Her defeated tone is pitiful.

"It's not funny!" She scolds. "He's worse than an actual child, and I'd know because I've babysat my nieces! They acted more obedient."

"Don't listen to her, Dasher. You're a good boy."

Fallon shakes her head, then puts her laptop down before standing. She sashays to the kitchen carrying the bag. "Where's your coffee maker?"

"Damn, I knew I was forgetting something," I mutter, keeping a straight face.

"Should've known it was too good to be true," she grinds out as she tries to walk past me.

I gently grab her elbow and pull her back in front of me. "I was kidding. Loosen up, *Fallon Joy.*"

Her eyes narrow before the corner of her lips slightly tilt up. "You're rude."

"And you're too serious," I say, moving into my pantry and grabbing the appliance from the top shelf. I went through a phase when I tried to drink it before work but never stuck with it. I'm naturally alert in the mornings anyway—a blessing when it comes to my job.

I set it on the counter and plug it in. When the clock flashes, I smile. "See, it might be old, but it still works."

"Like you?"

"You can't be that much younger than me."

"We'll see. I'm not celebrating until I have a hot cup in front of me."

"Just give me five minutes, and you'll be plenty satisfied."

Fallon snorts, and then I realize what I've said. "Only five minutes, huh?"

"Trust me, babe. I can last all night." I look up and meet her playful eyes.

"It's because you're a fuck *man*. Lots of practice, right?" Her serious tone has me bellowing out a laugh.

"And you know what they say about that? Practice makes perfect." I shoot her a wink.

And although she doesn't respond, I swear I see a hint of a blush covering her cheeks.

After everything's rinsed and situated, I press the brew button. Seconds later, coffee drips into the carafe.

Fallon looks like a kid in a candy store, and I don't think I've ever seen her smile this wide. Once it's finished, I grab a mug and fill it for her.

"I'm sorry I don't have any cream, but I have plenty of milk and sugar."

"Fine by me. I prefer it black anyway," she says.

"To match your *black heart*?"

"Yep," she deadpans.

Fallon takes a tiny sip because it's still really hot and moans. That sound has my cock twitching. I swallow hard, forcing my gaze away from her as she glances at me over the top of her mug. "It's exactly what I've been missing in my life."

"My mom has plenty more if you need it. That woman loves her coffee."

"She sounds way cooler than you," she taunts, hugging the ceramic with her hands.

"Yeah, I have a feeling you'll change your tune once you learn her love for Christmas is twice as intense as mine."

She makes a face, but then her lips curve into a smile as she blows on the liquid. "Right now, I don't care about anything other than drinking this."

Fallon grabs an ice cube from the freezer and puts it inside. Once it's cool enough to drink, she takes a big gulp and sighs.

"If this is all it took to make you happy, I would've jumped on the snowmobile four days ago."

Fallon playfully rolls her eyes, but when she looks at me, there's fire behind them.

I wish I knew why she continues to put on this hard-ass act because that's what it is. There are moments when her mask slips, and I see the real person hiding behind the scowl. She's more transparent than she thinks, but I'll continue to let her believe she has me fooled.

"Oh, before I forget. The furnace guy said he's booked up, so it might be a few days before he can come out."

"Great." She frowns.

"The other bit of bad news is there are no rooms available anywhere unless you want me to try the town over. But I suspect it's gonna be about the same."

"How far of a drive is it?"

"About fifty miles," I explain. "Could take over an hour to get from here to there, depending on if it's snowing or not."

"I don't want to keep imposing on your personal space. So if I have to drive an hour—"

"You can stay here, Fallon. I don't mind your company, even when you're a grumpy ass sometimes." I chuckle when she glares at me.

"Are you sure? I can—"

"Absolutely," I say. "Unless you want to leave? I can't imagine you'd have fun sleeping in that minivan."

"I don't *want* to leave," she admits, and it's music to my ears. "Honestly, I'd probably die of frostbite or be more miserable anywhere else. One of the reasons I agreed to come is because I'd have a large space to sleep and work."

"Well, I'd never let you freeze to death. You know my bed is always available whenever you need some extra warmth." I smirk.

Dasher trots over and interrupts us.

"Outside?"

He sprints toward the door and immediately flies off the deck. Once he does his business, he returns without issue. I know he was testing Fallon earlier.

"How'd you like your grinchy babysitter?" I ask, following him inside and getting a musky whiff of him.

Fallon is on the couch with her coffee and laptop.

"Gonna give Dasher a bath real quick. Need anything?"

"Nope, I'm good now."

Dasher's good and behaves for me while I wash him in the tub. He actually likes the warm water and is used to this routine since he gets them almost every day when it's wet or muddy outside. After he's scrubbed and rinsed, I lift him from the tub and towel dry him the best I can. I grab the hair dryer I have for him and use it until he's annoyed. As soon as I open the bathroom door, he bolts out.

Before I can call him or warn Fallon, he's sprinting downstairs.

"Hey!" Fallon shouts. "Get off me!"

Her helpful squeals make me laugh. "I'm jumping in the shower," I call down.

"Wait! Take your dog!" she shouts.

"Be right back!" I say, knowing she'll want to kill me later.

Turning on the water, I undress and then step underneath the hot stream. It cascades over my sore muscles, and I scrub both palms over my face and hair, trying to relax.

My cock grows hard as I reminisce about Fallon being in my bed last night. Though neither of us mentioned it, she snuggled up to me in her sleepy haze. I was up and out of bed before her, but I hardly slept as she pressed her ass against my cock and wiggled her body.

As I think about it, I reach down and roughly fist my dick. With my other palm pressed against the wall, my fantasies of Fallon naked in my bed take over.

I race in a full sprint toward the orgasm threatening to take over. Before

I can brace myself, the pleasure rips through me, and I groan out with relief.

My heart throbs as I look at the mess I've made. My come would look so stunning splashed across her beautiful breasts. It takes at least ten minutes before I come back to earth, even if she's still on my mind.

As I get out of the shower and then dry off, I wonder if she heard me. A part of me hopes she didn't, but then again, I'd own it if she did. It's nearly impossible to hide my attraction, especially when she looks at me like I'm dessert.

I'm ready to collapse from exhaustion, knowing I'll be just as busy tomorrow. I plan to show her exactly what our town has to offer, and I just hope it's enough to impress her.

CHAPTER NINE

FALLON

DAY 5

I ROLL over in Levi's bed, pulling the covers up to block out the sun. It was a middle-of-the-night decision that I might regret when I end up addicted to his touch. I shouldn't enjoy pressing my body against his for warmth, but I do.

Each time he pulls me against his chest, I remind myself that this is only temporary and not to get attached. Truthfully, I haven't slept this good in what feels like decades. We may start on separate sides of the mattress, but eventually, he covers me with his warmth and holds me tight.

Regardless, none of it changes the fact I'm leaving in nine days. I'll go home and finish my article, it'll be published, and I'll put this whole Christmas adventure behind me. I just hope my boss understands the sacrifices I've made to save this story when it's time for a promotion. He knows I want the senior editor position more than anything.

I give up trying to fall back to sleep and force myself out of bed. Once I'm dressed, I go downstairs, where smells of freshly brewed coffee waft through the air. I quickly make my way to the kitchen where a shirtless Levi stands in front of the stove. Dasher's in his usual position, begging at his feet. And as much as I don't want to admit it, I've already fallen in love with that spoiled fur ball.

Levi notices me and offers me a cup of coffee with a smile. "Good morning."

"Same to you."

I sit at the bar as he cooks.

"Are you excited to get out today? I thought I'd show you around the family farm and introduce you to everyone. Give you a proper tour around the place."

"Can't wait," I say because I'm going somewhat stir-crazy. However, I'm not looking forward to the holiday spirit being shoved down my throat all day.

Levi and I quickly eat. After checking the forecast, I decide to add more layers. I make sure my boots are tied securely around my ankles because the last thing I need is to bust my ass on the ice and snow.

After I slide on my gloves, we head toward the Christmas tree farm with Dasher in tow. The roads are cleared now, and I notice how much snow is piled on the sides. Proof I made the right decision to leave the airport.

I stare at the large pines that line the hillside and the fog that hovers above the ponds we pass. Once we arrive at the farm, I plan to take some photos for the article. I capture a few pictures with my phone and quickly review them, knowing it would make a beautiful postcard. It'd probably have some Christmas phrase underneath it like—*Dashing through the Snow* or *'Tis the Season to be Merry*. I laugh at the thought.

"What's funny?" Levi asks as Dasher lies on me.

"Just thinking how cliché everything is here. It almost doesn't seem real."

"Is that a good or a bad thing?" he asks hesitantly.

"That's still to be determined," I admit. "When my first flight was delayed, I googled the town. I remember thinking about how the pictures looked like a classic movie green screen. Now that I'm here and viewing it with my own eyes, it's surprisingly...*breathtaking*."

"It is, but I think sometimes I take it all for granted. Though I couldn't imagine being stuck in a city when places like this exist in the world."

I contemplate his words, but I'm too stubborn to admit he's right. "But there's delivery," I say, "*even* if there's snow."

Levi laughs. "I guess that's true, but Seattle's measly six-inch average is nothing in comparison. So tell me what you like most about living there and don't say delivery."

"Why? Thinking about moving to the city, country boy?"

"Country *man*. Trust me when I say there is no *boy* here," he puffs out his chest, and his gruff voice has me swallowing hard. I know more than anything he's *all man*. My gaze trails from the scruff on his chin to his plump lips until I eventually meet his blue eyes.

"You were saying?" The cocky smirk on his face makes me forget what we were even talking about.

I stutter, trying to find my words as I notice the bulge in his jeans. Maybe his cock likes my attitude after all. Getting under his skin has been some of the hottest foreplay I've experienced in a long time. I nervously laugh as I remember how hung he is. And he wasn't even hard.

"I don't remember what we were talking about," I mutter, just as my phone vibrates. I thank my lucky stars that my sister has come to my rescue.

"Hey!" I answer, my voice an octave higher than usual.

"Did I interrupt something?" she suspiciously asks.

"What? No."

"You're not having sex with the hot lumberjack?" she whispers like he might hear her. And hell, maybe he can, considering he's sitting two feet from me.

"No. Absolutely not," I say, quickly glancing at him.

"And why not? Sounds like a spicy Hallmark movie in the making. Go jump on that."

"Jesus Christ, Taryn. What do you want?" I ask, trying to keep my voice level as Levi glances over at me.

"Nothing. I was just thinking about you. Wanted to check in and see how things were going with your roommate and work."

"We're going to his family's Christmas tree farm. I've started on my article, but I'm still thinking about the story aspect."

"Maybe the grinch whose heart grew ten sizes?" she muses. "Nah, that's already been done. My vote is you should write about the girl who fell in love with a burly lumberjack during a blizzard. Think of the sales boom!"

"Okay, sis. Gotta go. Love you."

She bellows out a loud laugh. "Love you too!"

I hang up, hoping Levi doesn't see the embarrassment that's flushed my cheeks. Regardless, I'll have to thank her for that save.

We turn onto the main road that leads to the Christmas tree farm. A big hand-painted sign with a giant red arrow points toward the farm a mile away. Eventually, we pass an overflow lot and continue farther until we park in front of the shop. It looks like it came straight from Hogwarts with its dark rustic wood, high beams, and large windows that neatly frame the front porch. The smell of freshly baked chocolate chip cookies wafts through the air as smoke from a fireplace inside puffs from the chimney.

My mouth falls open with amazement as I take it in. Not wanting to forget a single detail, I snap several photos. Levi stands to the side with Dasher and watches me, allowing me time to capture everything I need. When I'm done, he leads me forward and opens the door for me.

"I'm going to put Dasher in the office while we walk around," he tells me, leaving me on my own in the packed shop. The sounds of laughter and chatter fill the space as carols play overhead. A fifteen-foot brightly lit Christmas tree is the focus in the center of the room, and behind it is a large brick fireplace that I'd expect to see at a ski resort. A few people stand close to it, warming their hands.

I study the beautiful painting of the snowy Christmas tree farm that's hanging behind the counter. It looks so realistic as if I could transport myself into the scene. My attention travels to the older woman ringing up customers, and I immediately know she's Levi's mother. They have the same kind eyes and smile. As soon as she spots me, she waves and makes a beeline toward us.

"You must be Fallon Joy!" She greets me like I'm an old friend of the family and wraps me in a hug. I awkwardly hug her back, not used to people being so friendly. I typically stay in my bubble.

"Yes, I am. You must be Mrs. White."

"Call me Eloise. It's lovely to meet you. I've heard so much about you."

"Nothing good, I'm sure."

She chuckles. "All great things," she reassures me, but her tone holds a hint of amusement.

"Mom." Levi returns. "I see you found Fallon."

"You didn't tell me she was gorgeous, Levi."

My cheeks heat at how sweet she's being.

"Didn't I? Must've slipped my mind," he deadpans.

"Has my son been treating you well?"

"Yes, he has. Oh, I wanted to thank you for the coffee. It was greatly appreciated and so delicious."

"Anytime. I keep a stockpile in the house if you need more. You should come visit sometime."

"Thank you. You're too nice. Why couldn't I have been scammed into walking into your house, instead?" I muse with a chuckle.

Levi rolls his eyes. "Why? So you could mace my poor old parents, instead?"

"*Levi Christmas White.* Who are you calling old?" she hisses with a popped brow.

"Please tell me your middle name is *not* Christmas…" I snicker.

"It's not." He shakes his head.

"No? Must've forgotten in my *old* age. Should've been, though. I missed out on a perfect opportunity." Eloise shrugs.

"I wouldn't have survived middle school," Levi mutters.

The line at the counter backs up, and Mrs. White notices. "Better get back to it. If you'd like anything from the shop, it's a gift from the family. Please help yourself."

"Thanks," I say. "You spoil me."

She pats me on the shoulder, then excuses herself.

"She's very sweet," I tell Levi. She reminds me of my mother, but I keep that to myself.

"Don't let her fool you. She has a bossy side," he taunts.

"I find that hard to believe."

"C'mon, let's go show you around." Levi grabs my hand, leading me around the shop before we stop for hot cocoa.

"Whipped cream?" he asks.

I nod, and he hands me a mug. "Wow." I take a sip.

"It's made with sweet chocolate and fresh milk. The whip is handmade too, none of that store-bought stuff."

"You should try one of our gingerbread snaps. They're kind of a big deal in the area."

The woman running the small concession just pulled a tray out of the oven, and I don't think I can say no even though I might pay for it later.

I'm handed one wrapped in a candy cane-striped napkin. It's still warm.

It smells like pure molasses, and I take a small bite. The flavors of sugar and spice explode in my mouth. To say I'm impressed by how delicious it is is an understatement. "Incredible. Really," I tell him, covering my mouth while I finish chewing.

"Is this me winning you over...one cookie at a time?" Levi waggles his brows, and I roll my eyes.

"Keep dreaming."

Once we finish the shop tour and I've downed my drink, Levi guides me toward the gift-wrapping area with a line to the door.

"Lucy," Levi calls, and I see a woman who looks just like him but with softer features. She's beautiful with dark-red lips and curly brown hair. "This is Fallon, the journalist."

"Oh, hi," she says, brushing loose strands of hair behind her ear. "Nice to meet you. I'm his twin sister—also known as the cool one."

"*Twins*? Well, now I have a lot of questions," I say.

"Don't worry, I'll spill *all* his secrets later when we hang out." Lucy's lips curve up into a smirk just as Levi's smile fades.

He places his arm on my shoulders and pretends to lead me away. "And now it's time to go."

"But it was just getting good!" I say. Levi moves his hand and turns back toward his sister. "I know you're really busy. We'll plan something and meet up later, for real, so you guys can chat."

"Oh, I know," she tells him. "Have fun, you two." She waggles her brow like she knows something I don't.

I give her a smile as Levi leads me down a long hallway. He opens a door, and Dasher wakes up, rushing to greet us.

We take a side exit to avoid the crowd and use a sidewalk that leads to the tree farm's entrance.

"So how's it work?" I ask.

"Well, you can either chop down your own tree or have one of our workers help cut it with a chainsaw. Either way, one of our guys drives around on a four-wheeler and will come and tag it. Then you pick it up at the front once it's been wrapped and ready to go. A lot of people just visit and stroll around because it's a fun environment. They like to browse the shop and try the samples."

"Wow. That sounds cool. Looks like you found your own way of making things more efficient." Dasher runs around, playing. His tongue eats up the snow as Levi tells him to stop it.

"Yeah, but we still try to keep the tree-picking experience as authentic as possible, too. It's why we offer axes for people who want to chop it manually. Makes it like it was back in the day when the farm first opened. I honestly think that's why we've been so successful over the decades."

I open the notepad app on my phone and jot down a few things. "I can quote you on whatever you say about this place, correct?"

He nods. "Absolutely."

We make our way down a well-maintained trail until we arrive at a live tree section. I notice how many stumps there are—hundreds—just in this small area.

"Are there other farms like this around here?" I ask.

"Next one is about a hundred miles, but it's not even close to our magnitude. Coming here has become a tradition for many families, and people drive from all around to visit. Apparently, it's an influencer favorite too. My sister runs our social media. I'll ask her what hashtags they're using. I don't pay much attention to it, and things are always changing."

"If you could get that info for me, that would be great. I'll have to do more research and see what I find." I continue typing on my phone, noting to look that up.

Once we reach the end of the long row, a teenage girl on a four-wheeler passes us and waves. I'm actually shocked at how many people are out here, considering Christmas is in less than two weeks.

"Is it typical for trees to be purchased this late in the season?"

"Oh yeah. We stay open through December twenty-third, and we'll be this busy until the minute we close. Then I have some time off and won't work again until after the new year."

"Really? What do you plan on doing?" Dasher doesn't leave my side.

He arches a brow. "I dunno how to break this to you, Fallon. I'm Santa and have to travel around the world to deliver gifts."

I chuckle. "You're ridiculous."

"And you're on the naughty list."

It's impossible for me to hold back my smile. "Sounds like you've got me all figured out, Levi."

"Oh, I know I do," he confidently says, picking up a stick and tossing it for Dasher, who bolts after it.

"When does the season start?"

"We work year-round. From late February to mid-April, we plant seedlings to regenerate the trees we cut. But tourist season ramps up in mid-October when we begin shipping trees to our wholesalers around the country. We open to the public on November first and work our asses off for eight weeks straight. We make enough money to keep the farm running throughout the year while we're doing farm maintenance, replanting, and shearing. A lot goes into it. The shop has been my mom's passion project for decades and now stays open year-round. And yes, the theme is Christmas all the time."

"This doesn't surprise me." I continue asking as many questions as I can. "How long does it take a tree to get to this size?" We pass one that's taller than me.

"About seven to eight years."

"Wow. And how long has this farm been here?"

Levi chuckles at my amazement. "About a hundred and twenty-three years."

"That's really…impressive."

"Yeah, you could say my love for Christmas has been passed down through the generations."

"Guess that explains all the decorations in your house," I add.

"Absolutely. We don't ever get rid of ornaments. But what's cool about the town is how the surrounding farms have become a part of the local culture. We bring in a lot of tourists around the holidays. My best friend's family's apple orchard celebrated its centennial last year, and it was a huge deal."

"Really? Will I be able to see it?"

"Yeah. I can set something up with Finn's grandma, Willa. I think you'll like her a lot. Then I can introduce you to him and his girlfriend, Oakley."

"That sounds perfect." I appreciate his help and him sharing all this knowledge with me. When I finally meet his blue eyes, butterflies swarm in my stomach. I turn my head, breaking the electrical current streaming between us.

We finally return to the shop and tell Levi's family goodbye before we go to the truck. Dasher sits between us, staring out the window. On the way out, we pass a horse pulling a sleigh full of people, and the driver waves at Levi, who returns the gesture.

Levi spends hours driving me around the farm, showing me the different areas of operation. I'm amazed by how much goes into this between planting and harvesting. He shows me his parents' house and points out which window was his room growing up, then takes me to his sister's. A lot of employees live on the property as well.

"I can't believe how large the place is." I take countless pictures of the scenic views so I can send them to my boss and show Taryn.

"Sometimes, I can't either," he admits.

Once I've seen most of it, we head back to his cabin. My stomach growls so loud, he hears it.

"Should we get a pizza? They have gluten-free. And we'll do beef. No pepperoni."

I nod. "Works for me."

He pulls his cell phone from his pocket and places an order. We pass his driveway, and I realize we're driving toward town. He parks in front of a pub on the corner of Main Street. "I'll be right back. Unless you want to tag along?"

I chuckle because he knows damn well I'm staying in the heated truck. "I'll stay and keep Dasher company."

He smiles, then quickly walks toward the building. Five minutes later, he returns with an extra-large box. I take it from him, not minding the warmth of it on my lap as we drive back.

Once we're inside, I set the pizza on the counter, and Levi grabs us plates.

I put a few slices on mine and so does he.

"Mm," I moan around a large bite. "This is so good."

He nods. "Yeah, I've never tried this crust, but it's not bad at all. They make really great hot wings too. It's the closest thing we have to fast food."

Levi snags a fourth piece, and I grab another too. Dasher stays at my feet as if he's hoping the cheese will slide off the top and land in front of him.

"Thanks again for showing me around today. It was fun learning about what you and your family do."

"You're welcome. I'm glad you enjoyed yourself. Showing you around is a welcomed distraction."

"I'm looking forward to getting to know your mom and sister more. They seem sweet and down to earth."

"They are. Most everyone is, though. We're a community and look out for one another."

I nod, seeing it as a small-town perk.

After we finish eating, he kicks off his boots, then sits on the couch. As he reaches for the remote, I speak up.

"Do you mind if I use your tub?"

"As if you need to ask. You basically live here," he teases, flipping through the channels.

"Ha ha. Well, just making sure you don't plan on barging in naked again."

"I mean, I can make that happen for ya," he tells me as I go upstairs to grab my things. I draw the water as I undress, then step in, sinking under the warmth.

With my eyes closed, I allow my imagination to wander as I envision Levi's lips nibbling on my ear and neck. My hand slides between my thighs as my body begs for a release. When I touch my swollen bud, I moan in anticipation. My pussy clenches as I insert one finger inside. As much as I want his touch, I know I'm terrible at choosing men. The last thing I need is to get my heart broken again, which would be inevitable since we live thousands of miles apart. I can't deny how things have changed between us since I first arrived.

I move back to my clit, which grows sensitive with each circle I make. I steady my pace, wishing his mouth and tongue were all over me as he breaks me with his huge cock. My erratic breathing fills the bathroom as I greedily race to the finish line.

"Fuck," I murmur as I climb closer to the edge, wishing I could feel his hot breath between my thighs as he devours my pussy. *Oh God*. I want him to talk dirty to me in his rough growly voice and wrap my hair tightly around his fist. A long moan echoes off the wall as I lose myself. As I come, I insert two fingers to ride out the wave.

Levi gets me so fucking worked up that I greedily want another. No man has ever captured my attention so quickly. I know we have nothing in common, but they say opposites attract. There's something sexy about the way he looks at me—as if he wants to trace every inch of my skin with his tongue and teeth. It makes me wonder if our chemistry would ever be enough for something more. He hasn't even kissed me, and my skin burns whenever he touches me.

I move back to my clit, teasing myself for this one. With my free hand, I pinch my nipple and tug on it, enjoying the pain mixed with pleasure. I almost wish he knew what he does to me and how wild he drives me. I groan, feeling the build come alive once again. I slide deeper into the tub, spreading my legs wider as I finger fuck myself to oblivion. My breasts rise and fall as I nearly gasp out his name in satisfaction.

I lie in the water staring at the ceiling until it fades from hot to warm. A part of me wants to know what he's like in bed—a bad boy with a dirty mouth or a delicate lover who's passionate and sweet. If I got to choose, I'd want a perfect mixture of both. A man who will fuck me until I'm sore, who enjoys me choking on his cock, but isn't afraid to stare into my eyes and admit how much he loves me.

I almost laugh because what are the odds that man actually exists?

However, I think with Levi's experience, he'd be the one to teach me a thing or two. Unfortunately, I'm too stubborn to admit I'm attracted to the man who loves Christmas just as much as I hate it.

Apparently, he's just as chickenshit as I am. His thick erection while I sleep next to him tells me he *really* likes me near him.

When the water turns cold, I climb out and wrap a towel around me. I catch a glimpse of myself in the mirror and study my naked body. My shitty ex made me feel disposable, as if I'd never be good enough. Levi, on the other hand, looks at me like I'll disappear if he blinks. Sometimes I catch him staring, and he makes me feel sexy.

If I could get over my trust issues and make a move, I would because I deserve to be happy, too. Whether that's temporary or possibly something that could be long-term. Regardless, I'll never know if I stay guarded. Secluding myself from everyone is all I've known because it's easier.

Once I'm dry and have wrapped my hair in a towel, I open the bathroom door to find Levi. He's standing with his back to me and a towel wrapped around his waist.

He must've just finished showering in the other bathroom because drops of water trace down the muscles of his back. Before I can announce myself, he drops the towel, giving me the perfect view of his ass.

"Shit, sorry," I say, flustered and frozen in place.

He pays me no attention. "Nothing you haven't seen before, Fallon."

"I gather you're actually not shy," I muse, drinking him in just a little bit longer.

He slips on some joggers, then looks at me. "If you weren't here, I'd probably walk around naked."

"Well, don't let me stop you. Just give me a warning when your reindeer and jingle bells are loose." My eyes trail down to the outline of his cock pressing against the material of his pants. I swallow hard at the thickness.

He licks his lips as my gaze travels up his happy trail and abs to his eyes. Yeah, I'm definitely busted.

I briefly lose my ability to speak and force out a good night before moving past him. I needed to get the hell out of his room before I did something stupid.

"Night," he calls out with amusement in his voice.

Once I'm in my room, I settle in my bed with my laptop. I work on transferring the notes from my phone into my document. An hour later, I can't keep my eyes open.

I shut everything off and slide deeper under the pile of blankets. My body begs for sleep, but I roll around for at least an hour. I try to count down from a hundred to zero *twice*. It doesn't work.

Instead of fighting it any longer, I get up and make my way into Levi's room. Dasher's head pops up as soon as I tiptoe inside. Without a word,

Levi lifts the blankets like he's been expecting me. I don't hesitate and climb in. As soon as he covers us up, I mold my body against his, settling my ass against his groin.

He wraps his strong arm around my waist and leans into my ear. "Fuck, you smell so goddamn good."

His warm breath tickles against my neck, and I hold back a smile. He holds me tighter, warming me from the inside out, and I feel safer than I've ever felt before.

Being in his protective embrace relaxes me as I close my eyes. It only takes a few minutes to fall asleep—a comfort I'll miss when I leave.

CHAPTER TEN

LEVI

DAY 6

WAKING up with Fallon's body pressed to mine is sweet torture. Her body wash and shampoo consumed my senses all night while her ass rubbed against my dick, making me hard. It was nearly impossible to fall asleep.

But I refused to move because her soft snoring made me smile. It was the only time she wasn't running her mouth or talking shit about Christmas, so I soaked it in until I drifted off.

Not to mention, I'd never pass up the opportunity to hold her.

Getting to know Fallon over the past five days has been a roller coaster of emotions. We constantly go back and forth between annoying each other and growing closer. This thing between us has been brewing since the day she arrived, and now we're playing a game to see who will snap first. However, she's the one who initiates sleeping in my bed, so I think I might be winning.

As soon as she woke up this morning, she climbed out of my bed and went to her room as if our night snuggling never happened. She doesn't mention it, so I don't push the conversation.

Most women are eager for my attention and nearly beg to spend a night in my bed, but not Fallon. No, she acts as if she only wants me for my warmth, but I know better.

She's constantly fighting this attraction between us. If she'd allow it, I'd prove to her that the feelings were mutual.

After we eat, we hop in the truck for a new day of activities.

"It looks so different with all the surrounding hills covered in snow," she says, practically pressing her face against the truck window. "Almost magical."

"Have we captured your heart already? I've hardly shown you anything," I taunt, glancing over at how beautiful she looks today.

"I never doubted the scenery was gorgeous," she counters. "I'll decide on the rest once I meet more people and hear some of their stories."

"Have you figured out what you'll write about my family's farm?"

"Not yet, but considering I've had an insider's view and learned some of the history, I'll probably start there. I plan on integrating the other businesses and farms into the story too."

"I left a message for the mayor so you can meet him personally before the festival. Until then, I'll show ya around, and you'll learn all the things in no time. But first, I want to show you Oakley's painting hung in the town hall. Then we'll stop for lunch."

"So when can I meet Finn and Oakley?" she asks, and I love that she sounds genuinely interested.

"I chatted with Willa this morning. We're going to stop by on Sunday, and I told them we'd visit after seeing the inn." That gives us two days.

She nods as I park in front of the diner right in the downtown square.

"Well, I can't deny it's giving me Christmas Hallmark vibes with a side of mountain rustic."

I tug on the strings of her hat and smirk. "Please tell me that's the name of the article."

She rolls her eyes, batting my hand away. "You'll find out once I'm done."

"I don't even get a sneak peek?"

"We'll see..." she taunts, bracing herself for the cold air before I hop out of the truck and open her door.

"Fuck." She shivers.

"At least the sun is out." I smirk, resting a palm on the small of her back as I guide her down the sidewalk.

"Well, it must be for show only because it's not warming up a damn thing," she groans, and I chuckle at her dramatics.

The town hall building is a few blocks away, and she soaks in the heat as soon as we enter. "Now this is what I'm talking about."

"When Oakley arrived here last fall, she was hired to paint a canvas of Bennett's Orchard Farm for the centennial celebration. Once the mayor saw it, he begged her to stay and paint one of the annual fall festival," I explain as we admire the large canvas proudly displayed on the wall.

"Wow..." Her eyes scan over every inch. "Look at those colors."

"There's nothing like seeing Vermont in the fall," I say. "When we visit, I'll show you the painting she did for the Bennetts. She nailed the orange and red trees that line the hillside behind the original buildings on the farm."

"So Oakley ended up staying after her projects were finished?" she asks as we make our way toward the diner.

I chuckle. "No. She actually left."

Fallon looks confused, so I continue.

"Her entire life was in LA, but after a couple of weeks, she came back to tell Finn she didn't want to live without him. They've been together ever since."

"Wow. Sounds like a movie." Fallon is quiet for a moment. "I bet leaving the city was a huge change for her."

"I think it was at first, but she's settled in just fine. Now she does most of her artwork online and gets commissioned for paintings from businesses all over. She sometimes travels on the weekends for special projects but not often. They're still in that honeymoon phase when they can't keep their hands off each other. They're actually perfect for one another."

"Hmm...that's an adorable story the magazine would eat up."

"Vermont orchard brings two unlikely people together in a whirlwind romance for the ages..." I say. "Found your title."

"Geez. You want my job, too?"

Laughing, I shake my head as I open the door to the diner, and we walk in.

"I'll leave that to the expert," I tease.

"Oakley painted that one in the shop behind the counter."

"She did that one too? I couldn't stop admiring it yesterday."

"Yeah! She's great. If I remember correctly, she's supposed to paint at the Christmas tree lighting during the winter festival this season. Each year, my family donates the massive tree that will be lit to kick off the celebration."

"Really?" She whips out her phone and starts typing into her notes.

"Yeah, they've done that for as long as I can remember. You'll find that many of the local traditions are supported by the farms or small businesses. We all come together to make it special because this place means so much to us."

"Well, if it isn't *Levi White*," Greta singsongs. She's owned the diner for as long as I can remember.

"Greta, my favorite lady." I hug her, and she squeezes me in return.

"You brought a guest?" She glances next to me, her brow arched in question.

"Yes, this is Fallon Joy. She's a journalist from Seattle doing a holiday tourism piece for a magazine. I'm showing her around."

"Lovely to meet you, Fallon. I'm Greta. Welcome to our small town." She holds out her hand, and Fallon takes it.

"Nice to meet you, too. Your diner is very charming."

"Thanks." She beams.

I have to give it to Fallon for how quickly she turns on the charm.

"Let's get you two to a booth. I'm sure you're hungry," Greta tells us, grabbing menus and leading the way. Fallon glances at the Christmas tinsel, mini trees, and ridiculous amount of colorful lights that fill the small place. I know she's cringing inside

Once we sit, Greta asks for our beverage order.

"I'll have a lemonade," Fallon says.

"Me too."

Greta nods before walking away.

"She seems nice," Fallon mutters, focusing on the menu. I already know what I want, so I don't bother looking.

"She is. She also knows all the town gossip and is in everyone's business."

"Really? Even yours?" She drops the menu and smirks.

"*Everyone's*," I emphasize.

"Well, I might have a few questions for her, then."

"Here you kids go." Greta sets our drinks on the table, takes our order, then leaves again.

"You're already living in my house and sleeping in my bed. Plus, you've already seen me naked. What more could you possibly want to know?" I ask, barely above a whisper.

She swallows hard, her cheeks paint into a beautiful shade of pink. Fallon doesn't get deep with people or share personal things about herself often, that much I've learned.

"Have you ever been married before?" she asks, and I blink in surprise at the random question.

"No. Why?"

She takes a sip of her lemonade. "Just trying to figure out why a thirtysomething man—with a stable job, a nice house, lots of land, and from what I can tell, no murder experiencing—can still be single. And before you feed me the bullshit of how you haven't found *the one*, I have a gut feeling there's more to it than that. Perhaps Greta can fill in the gaps for me?"

The compliments she rambled off amuse the hell out of me. Even if she threw a couple of jabs in the very next breath.

Shrugging, I grab my lemonade and take a drink. "I'm thirty-five. You act like I'm too old to still get married or something, but I don't know what to tell ya. I've never felt a spark outside the bedroom that has made me want more."

"I'm only thirty and am already sick of the dating scene because of men who *only* want hookups. I can't imagine what it'll be like in five years." She makes a face as if the thought of dating disgusts her. "Have you ever tried getting to know someone before jumping into bed with them?"

I'm tempted to tell her that she's the first, but when Greta slides our plates onto the table, I pause.

"Let me know if you need anything else," she says, and Fallon doesn't hesitate to stop her.

"Actually, I was hoping to pick your brain a little."

Greta smiles wide. "Ask away, sweetie."

"What kind of guy is Levi White?"

Confusion is written all over Greta's face.

"Well, let me explain. I ended up at his cabin by accident as the blizzard rolled in, which meant I was stuck there. Do you find it odd that this man would just let a strange woman live in his house?"

Greta listens intently, and I know she's adding Fallon's story to her gossip list.

Although they're talking about me like I'm not here, I speak up. "Feel free to answer truthfully. I actually want to hear this."

Greta turns her attention back to Fallon as I brace myself. "Well, it's not surprising he'd help a stranger, especially in the middle of a storm. Levi would give the shirt off his back to someone if they needed it. I'd consider yourself lucky that you ended up at his house instead of someone else's. On the flip side, I think you're the first woman who's ever stayed there for more than one night in a row."

And there it is. She started out so strong.

"Interesting..." Fallon grins. "Are you surprised he's never been married?"

"Levi?" Greta bellows out a laugh. "Oh, sweetie, no. Be careful using that word around him, though. You might scare the Christmas spirit out of him."

"Oh, c'mon," I groan, picking up my sandwich. "You act like I have a commitment phobia."

"What would you call it?" Greta asks with a hand on her hip. Fallon smirks at the way she grills me.

"Someone who doesn't settle for anything less than what he deserves."

Fallon rolls her eyes, digging into her food. "Pretty sure my ex said the same thing to me when he refused to be exclusive."

As soon as the words fly out, she quickly covers her mouth. "Shit, I hadn't meant to say that."

"And the truth comes out."

"Forget I mentioned it."

Unlikely.

Greta is pulled away to help another customer while Fallon and I eat in awkward silence. There's no denying that her ex is why she's reluctant to get into a relationship. Not that I'm actively searching, but when the universe drops a brunette bombshell in your bed, you don't pass up the opportunity to see if she's *the one*.

Once we're done eating, I grab the check, and we head to the register. The door swings open, and Catharina strolls in with one of her friends—whose name I can't remember.

"Levi!" she squeals, nearly pushing Fallon to give me an *unwanted* hug. "How are you? It's been *so* long."

"Hi, Catharina."

"You remember my friend Gabby?"

"Of course," I say, playing it off.

"Who's this?" Catharina asks, giving Fallon a not-so-subtle death glare.

"Fallon Joy. I'm a journalist here on business. Levi's just showing me around," Fallon says.

"How wonderful!" Catharina gushes, but I don't miss Fallon's clenched jaw. "You're so lucky to have a strong man like Levi to be your tour guide, especially in this weather."

"Yeah, I feel so damn lucky," Fallon states with sarcasm lacing her words. Her serious tone has me holding back a laugh.

"Well, it was great seeing you again. Give me a call sometime!"

Once I tip Greta, I lead Fallon outside and breathe in the cool air.

"Where to next, *oh holy guide*?" She rolls her eyes as we stroll down the sidewalk.

I chuckle and take her hand. "Better plaster on that fake smile again. We're about to meet all the small business owners on this block."

It takes two hours to introduce Fallon to everyone, from the gift shops to the movie theater and the hotel—they talk her ear off until I literally have to drag her away. When we reach the end of the street, she's socially exhausted.

"Doing okay?"

"I've heard enough about Christmas for one day. I'm at my max."

"That's fine. Just need to run to the grocery store before we head home. I'm sure the mayor will also take you around when you meet up with him."

"Great." There's zero enthusiasm in her voice as we drive to the store.

As we go inside, I tell her to pick out whatever she wants since her choices have been limited.

Once we get a cart, a woman speaks from the checkout. "Hey, Levi."

"Hello, Mrs. Shrader," I greet, waving to her as Fallon leads us down an aisle.

"Levi, hey." Cassie stops me as I reach for a box of snack cakes. "Haven't seen you at the pub in a while."

"Hi, Cass. It's my busy season," I explain.

"Oh yeah, I almost forgot that you disappeared during the holidays. We'll have to catch up after New Year's and shoot some pool. Drinks on me."

"Great," I mutter, not wanting to be rude. However, I'm not excited about her offer.

"See ya soon," she calls out as I catch up with Fallon.

"Finding what you need?" I ask her.

"Came across some gluten-free bread and flour tortillas for chicken wraps. Now I just need some avocados," she mentions without looking at me.

"Sounds good. I need to run to the back of the store for some things. I'll meet you in the produce section."

"Alright."

We go our separate ways. Hopefully, this will help speed things up. I manage to grab a dozen eggs and some butter, then make my way back to Fallon.

"Levi." I hear someone say my name, and I stop in my tracks. When I turn, I see Presley with her hands on her hips.

"I haven't heard from you. Why is that?" She pouts like she's hurt, but there's a flirty grin on her face.

We spent one night together *two years ago*. I told her I wasn't interested in anything more, but she constantly finds a way to bring it up.

"Been staying busy on the farm," I say, my go-to response anytime someone complains about me not being around. It's not a lie, though. I've worked every day for the past two months, other than the three when I was snowed in.

"Well, hopefully I'll see you at the festival. I'll buy you an eggnog." She smiles wide and lifts a brow. More like *spiked* eggnog.

"I'll be there," I tell her. The whole damn town will be.

When I finally meet up with Fallon, she's comparing two zucchinis.

"The left one has more length if you're into that. But the right one has more girth. Tough decision," I taunt, standing behind her.

"Too bad a girl can never find the right one..."

I meet her eyes and smirk.

"You know, one with length *and* girth. It's a rare find."

Now I know she's messing with me because she's seen and felt my dick on more than one occasion.

"Anytime I've found one that's long and thick, it always turns out terrible." She lifts a brow. "No flavor."

"That's an odd observation," I state.

She tosses both in the cart. Then she gives me her signature death glare. "What took you so long? Get stopped by another fan club member?"

Her jealous tone makes the corner of my lips curl up. "It's a small town. I told you, everyone knows everyone."

"I guess I hadn't realized you meant it *literally.* "

"Why don't you just ask me what you want to know? Stop beating around the bush and just say it."

"Nah, I'm good." She moves over to the fruit.

I wait in silence as she picks out apples and oranges, then I follow her to the yogurt section. Once she's finished, we make our way to the cashier.

"Hi, Levi," Sierra greets sweetly as I put things on the belt. I glance over at Fallon, who's rolling her eyes.

Great. I'm sure she thinks I've hooked up with Sierra too, and that has never happened.

"Hey. How's your fiancé?" I ask. The douchebag just got out of jail last month for assault.

"He's fine, thanks for asking. How's your mom?"

We go back and forth until the cart is empty, and I introduce her to Fallon. Once I've paid and our groceries are bagged, we leave.

"You can sit in the truck and get warm while I load these," I tell her, cranking the heat.

She nods. I don't push her to talk, though, because she told me she was exhausted, and I want to respect her boundaries. I've always been a chatty guy—kinda comes with the territory—but I understand wanting peace and quiet.

We listen to soft non-holiday music as I drive home. She stares out the window, and I'm sure she fell asleep by how her head bobs.

"Fallon." I pat her thigh when I've parked in front of the cabin. "We're home."

She blinks over at me, waking up, and nods.

"Go ahead, and I'll bring in the bags."

Fallon jumps out and pulls up her hood as she walks across the snow. I follow her so I can unlock the door and let Dasher out. Just as she takes the first step, she slips, but I catch her before she busts her ass on the ice.

"Jesus. You okay?" I hold her tight as she finds her footing.

"Yeah, I think so."

"Sorry, I need to salt again."

I keep hold of her, not wanting to let go. "Are you sure you didn't twist or pull anything?"

She looks up at me and licks her lips as if she wants to say something but is holding back.

"No, I'm fine," she bites out, grabbing the rail and moving toward the door.

Once it's unlocked, Dasher flies toward us, and he comes outside with me.

I refuse to make more than one trip, so I haul all ten bags inside. It's a miracle I don't fall or drop anything. As soon as I set them on the counter, Fallon helps me unload them.

"So what do you want me to make with those zucchini?"

"Zucchini noodles. They're really good with tomatoes and garlic topped with parmesan cheese," she tells me, which explains the weird food we bought.

"I can make it tonight for you if you want? In fact, why don't you go lie down, and I'll finish here."

"You know how to make it?" she asks, yawning.

"No, but I know how to Google a recipe," I counter.

"Fine. But it's still cold in my room."

Jasper hasn't given me an update yet, so I assume he's still backed up.

"Sleep in mine. I'll build a fire for you, and you'll stay toasty warm."

"Thanks."

She heads upstairs, and I grab a few logs from the living room before meeting her.

Dasher follows and lies next to her on the bed.

"Alright, you should be good for a few hours. I'll wake you for dinner," I tell her, then snap my fingers for Dasher to come.

"He can stay," she murmurs, pulling the covers to her neck.

I arch a brow in surprise. "Okay."

By the time I finish putting away the groceries, my head is spinning. Fallon quickly shut down after talking to so many people, and I can't help but feel like it's my fault. We've been in our own little bubble for five days, so I didn't realize she wasn't overly social.

Perhaps a nap and a hot meal will help her recharge and put her in a good mood.

Well...one can hope.

CHAPTER ELEVEN

FALLON

I SNUGGLE into Levi's bed with the scent of him lingering on the blankets and relax. The heat of the fire smothers me in warmth, and I never want to leave this perfect sanctuary.

My mind wanders as I imagine what it'd feel like to sleep in Levi's arms and wake up in this bed every day for the rest of my life. I've only experienced it for a few nights, and I'm already addicted to the way I feel —safe and wanted.

His strong hand always snakes around my waist and then he grabs my hip. Having him hold me is a gesture I secretly crave.

In a sleepy haze, I think about how much I desperately want his hands and mouth on me. Every inch of him screams out that he's a man who definitely knows what he's doing.

While my heart knows it's irresponsible to have a short-term fling, my body wants to throw all reasoning out the window and experience his touch on every inch of me.

A phantom squeeze over my hip has me moaning out his name, and I seek more. I arch my back, wishing I could clear my doubts about his fuck *man* ways. By the multiple fan club members who begged for his attention today, I'm convinced he's exactly like my ex—unwilling to commit exclusively to one woman.

I feel it again and know in my fantasies, I'd let him slide his hand underneath my panties and discover how wet he makes me. Another whimper of a moan escapes me as I ache to feel the real thing.

Just as I'm about to widen my thighs and do the job myself, I feel his mouth press against my ear. "You moaning out my name in my bed is testing my willpower, Fallon. I have a lot of respect when it comes to boundaries, but you're making me hard as fuck right now."

My breathing grows erratic at the realization that his hand *is* tightly gripping my hip.

"What are you doing?" I whisper, embarrassed.

His facial hair scratches along my jaw and neck, his lips marking my skin along the way. "I came to wake you for dinner, but now all I can think about is devouring you instead."

My chest rises and falls, and there's no denying we're both worked up. His erection pushes into my lower back, and I fight the urge to turn and grasp it in my palm.

"What were you dreaming about?" he asks when I stay silent. "What was I doing to you?"

"I wasn't dreaming," I admit. "I was half asleep and *fantasizing* about your touch."

"And you liked it?"

"Maybe," I mutter. My heart explodes with each rushing beat it takes.

"I think you fucking *loved* it," he murmurs as his hand slides under my shirt. My breath hitches as the pads of his fingers rub circles along my bare skin.

"*Yes*," I whisper in a hushed tone because it's undeniable. "But now I'm more awake and aware of what's going on."

His hand freezes as it travels toward my breasts, and I almost beg him for more.

"I want to respect your boundaries, Fallon," he says, inching away and pulling me to my back so I'm forced to look at him. "But something is brewing between us. If it's not one-sided, then we owe it to ourselves to explore it further."

"I know," I whisper. "I just.." The rest of the words don't form, and I completely freeze.

Levi, being the perfect gentleman, gives me a sweet smile. "It's okay.

You need food and way more rest. Wake up a bit, then meet me downstairs."

He stands, adjusting himself, and I fall back in bed, elated but also mortified. I don't know what I said or what he saw. Once I compose myself, I make my way downstairs.

When I enter the kitchen, the hearty tomato aroma floats through the air, making my mouth water. Levi's standing at the stove making our plates. "What would you like to drink?"

"What are you having?" I ask.

He smirks over his shoulder with amusement. "Hard cider. Wanna try some? It's from Bennett's orchard and will help you stay warm."

"Yeah, that actually sounds good," I say, happy to have some alcohol to loosen me up.

"Wow, you did a good job," I say as he sets my food in front of me.

"Don't thank me just yet. Taste it first and let me know what you think."

I stare at his tight ass as he digs in the fridge for our drinks. Once he straightens, I snap my gaze to his.

"Thanks," I offer when he hands me a can.

I pop it open, take a sip, and am surprised by how sweet it is.

"I like it. Now for the real test."

I twirl the zucchini in my fork, then stab a couple of tomatoes.

"Here goes nothing," I tease, hoping to clear the tension in the air. I know a man like Levi isn't used to women hesitating, and I feel guilty for denying us both what we want.

"Oh my God..." I moan around a mouthful. "You nailed it."

"I found a video tutorial and did everything the same," he tells me proudly.

I take another bite, thinking about how good he is at following directions, and am curious if he's that way in the bedroom too. "I'm starting to wonder if there's anything you *can't* do."

"Oh there is..." He stands next to me while I sit at the breakfast bar so I'm only a few inches shorter than him. "Seduce you, for starters."

Ah, there's his hurt ego.

"That was you trying to seduce me?" I bite back a laugh, finding it cute that he has no idea how crazy he makes me.

He glares as if he's actually offended.

"It's probably because you've never had to try with anyone before. You snap a finger, and they come running." At the sound of me demonstrating, Dasher actually comes over. I'm almost shocked he listened, but then I laugh at the prime example. "You even have *him* trained."

He flashes a cocky smirk and spins the barstool until I face him. Then he leans down and rests both hands on either side of me, caging me into his arms. "I'm not gonna lie and say I don't like a good chase, but when you close me out because of something that happened in your past, it makes me want to prove to you that I'm not like that."

"I think at least thirty-eight women would disagree." I throw out the number he'd told me he'd been with. Whether or not that's true, I still don't know.

A wide grin covers his face as he scrubs a hand over his facial hair and inches closer.

"Fallon..." He says my name with pure sex on his tongue. "Can I kiss you?"

Instinctively, I lick my lips and inhale sharply. Having him kiss me is all I've thought about for the past three days, so now that he's asking and offering, I can't say no.

So I nod.

Slowly, he cups my face and rubs the pad of his thumb gently over my cheek, making my heart pound impossibly harder. The anticipation is almost too much as he takes his sweet time.

And then, finally, he brushes his mouth over mine.

I lean into him, giving him all of me as he dips his tongue between my lips. Deeper and deeper, he takes and takes, kissing me tenderly one moment, then savagely the next as if he'll die without the taste of me.

"Fallon," he growls, standing between my thighs. His erection jabs into my stomach, and it takes every ounce of my strength not to explore him.

"You taste even better than I imagined," he whispers, and I greedily want more. Instead, he releases me.

After taking the seat next to me, he spins my chair back toward my plate. "Don't want your food to get cold."

I glance over at him, wondering what he's thinking and why he stopped. It's not because he was worried about my dinner, but my stomach growls so I finish eating.

After ten minutes, he asks, "Want another?" He holds up my empty can, and I nod, hoping it'll help me relax since my nerves feel like they're on fire.

"Thanks," I say when he hands me a different flavor.

"That's my favorite one."

I look at the label. "Sour Apple," I read aloud, then try a sip. "Wow, it's delicious."

"Try mine. It's their seasonal flavor."

I take his can and read it. Cranberry.

After I take a drink, I nod in agreement. "Yum. That's good too."

"Be careful. These will get you fucked up without you even realizing," he teases, but I can tell he's serious. I can hardly taste the alcohol.

Once we've cleared our plates and he loads the dishwasher, we meet in the living room. He sets more logs on the fire, and we watch the flames dance in the dark.

"Wanna play a game?" he asks.

"Like Checkers?"

He chuckles. "No, like *Never Have I Ever* or *Truth or Dare*."

"Isn't that for teenagers?" I furrow my brow.

He shrugs. "Well, if you're too chickenshit, forget it."

I elbow him in the side. "I'm not! Let's play the first one, then."

I won't admit that the thought of playing *Truth or Dare* gives me hives. I know he'd come up with things I'd either not want to answer or do. So *Never Have I Ever* it is.

"Alright. If I say something I've never done but you have, you drink, and vice versa."

"Fair enough."

Not for *him* though. I can think of at least a hundred things I haven't done.

"Ladies first," he says, getting comfortable on the couch next to me.

I think for a quick moment. "Okay. Never have I ever had sex in a public place."

"Damn, woman. Going right for the jugular." He chuckles and takes a drink.

Why am I not surprised?

"My turn. Never have I ever broke into someone's house and slept in their bed."

I glare at him, tightly pursing my lips as realization dawns on me. He's here to deliver gut-punches and make sure I lose.

"That was low...*even for you.* I wasn't even asleep yet." I chug back the can. "And it wasn't even low-key breaking in. You left the door unlocked!"

"I doubt that excuse would fly with the police."

I roll my eyes, ready to play him at his own game.

"Never have I ever exposed myself to a complete stranger and flailed on the floor with my junk hanging out."

His tongue darts out as the curve of his mouth turns up. Then he takes a drink.

"I hope you know what you're doing. I'm the reigning champ of this game."

"Well...you *were*," I counter.

"Never have I ever masturbated in someone else's tub and loudly moaned."

I keep my gaze locked on his, determined not to admit that very thing.

How would he even know that? Unless he heard me moaning and saying his name?

"You're not drinking?" he asks with amusement in his eyes.

"I'm not sure I believe you. Surely, you've jerked off in a shower other than your own before."

"Well, that's why I said *tub,* sweetheart."

"I'm not drinking on a *technicality.*"

"Fine, we'll call a truce and both drink."

I lift my can, and he cheers it with his, then we both down the rest.

"Guess we need another." He stands to retrieve two more, letting me pick which flavor I want.

"Your turn," he tells me.

I swallow down my doubt and put on a brave face.

"Never have I ever..." I hesitate before forcing the words out. "Wanted someone as badly as I do right now after only knowing them less than a week."

He stares at me as if he's waiting for me to take a drink, but neither of us move.

"Your turn then," I say.

But instead, he locks his eyes on mine while chugging his drink.

And then I do the same.

Without a word, he grabs my can and puts both of ours down on the coffee table. Then he pulls me onto his lap to straddle him and presses his mouth to mine.

As his lips consume me, I wrap my arms around his neck and rock against the hard bulge between my thighs. He sucks on my tongue as I grind faster on him.

"You're playing with fire," he warns, cupping my ass and pushing up into me. The friction's a mix of warmth and desire.

"I want you, Levi," I finally admit as his mouth moves down my neck and toward my ear. "Now."

"On your knees, Fallon." His voice comes out in a low growl.

I immediately obey, positioning myself between his spread legs.

"Pull out my cock," he orders.

He lifts his hips so I can pull down his pants and boxers, and his dick springs free. I spit on it, then slowly stroke him from top to bottom.

"Fuck." He bucks his hips. "Take whatever you want, Fallon. I'm all yours."

As I look up at him, I feel powerful, knowing he's at my mercy. He's giving me the power to do whatever I want to him with no pressure or guilt.

I grip his thick shaft, admiring how much blood pumps as it aches for a release. Swiping my tongue up his thick vein, I land under the tip, and he hisses in response. I can't deny how much I like hearing him moan.

Pulling his crown between my lips, I hollow my cheeks and suck. My tongue slides around and tastes every delicious inch of him.

"My God, Fallon. You're driving me fucking crazy with that hot, greedy mouth of yours." He grabs my head, tangling his fingers in my hair as I continue to worship every long inch of him. I love having his soft, velvety skin between my lips. The ache between my thighs becomes unbearable as he hisses and groans out my name.

"You still planning to give me that pearl necklace?" I taunt when I come up for air, keeping my palm tightly wrapped around him.

"Fuck, sweetheart. It's all I've thought about. But not right now. I need to taste your cunt before I lose my goddamn mind."

Standing, I strip, knowing he's seen all of me already. As soon as I slip off my panties, he hauls me to the couch and settles me flat on my back.

"Jesus." I groan, needing him to hurry.

He removes the rest of his clothing before he spreads me wide and slides between my thighs.

Levi lifts my legs over his shoulders and swirls his tongue over my sensitive bud.

"Holy shit." The intense sensation has me writhing underneath him. No guy has ever been so willing to please me, and I never realized how amazing it could feel when a man enjoys eating pussy.

His breathy growls and wet kisses push me toward the edge fast and hard.

"Levi, right there..." I moan, arching my hips into him as he cups my ass and holds me steady.

Minutes, hours, days...I don't know how much time passes because the pleasure his mouth creates nearly makes me black out. His steady circular movements over my clit have me flying toward the cliff.

Everything shakes as my vision goes white, and I dig my nails into his shoulders. My chest tightens and expands as the hold on my orgasm releases.

"Oh my God," I finally breathe out, my limbs feeling like gelatin.

"Christ, baby. You came so damn hard." He wipes his chin with his forearm. "You taste so good. My new favorite flavor."

He crawls up my body, cupping my cheek and tenderly presses his lips to mine. His deep, rough voice calling me *baby* is enough to make me explode again.

"Are you okay?" He chuckles when I don't move.

Finally, I swallow and wet my lips. "That's never happened before," I admit.

He arches one brow. "You've never had an orgasm?"

"Not from oral," I explain. "Only from my fingers."

He stares at me with disbelief. "You're *joking*."

"I wish."

"Have you finished during sex?"

I lower my eyes and shake my head.

"That's not your fault." He tilts up my chin, forcing our eyes to meet. "You deserve better than that."

"I've not had the best of luck with dating," I confess. "I should've had higher standards, but I didn't always know what to look for."

"Higher standards? Where was the bar? *The floor*?"

I snort because he's not wrong. "You could say that."

"Alright, get up."

"What?" I ask, confused.

"I'm not letting a beautiful woman like you go without knowing what an orgasm feels like during sex. I hope you're ready because I'm going to blow your goddamn mind."

"You sound awfully confident," I taunt as he lifts me, then hauls me over his shoulder like a possessive mountain man. "Levi! Put me down!"

"For the next few hours, your body is mine, Fallon."

Hours?

Is he serious?

His hold on me tightens as he takes the stairs. "Levi...I can walk."

He chuckles. "You won't be saying that tomorrow."

I groan, kicking my feet. He locks his arm around me.

"You're about to see my possessive side, baby. We aren't leaving my bed until you've counted to five."

"Five? *Five what?*"

He smacks my ass as we go into his room, then tosses me onto the mattress. Levi hovers above me with his palms on either side of my head.

"Five mind-blowing, earth-shattering, tsunami-level orgasms."

I blink up at him. "I won't be able to move after that."

He winks, then lowers his mouth until his breath brushes over my flushed skin. "That's the point, sweetheart."

CHAPTER TWELVE

LEVI

As soon as I crash our lips together, she wraps her legs around my waist, and my erection throbs between her thighs.

Thighs that I very much want wrapped around me.

"I'm going to make you forget those so-called *men* ever existed," I warn, sucking on her soft skin. "I want every pathetic memory replaced with ones of you screaming out *my* name."

I palm her breast before pinching a nipple and enjoy the way she yelps in pleasure.

"Levi..."

"Yes, just like that, sweetheart."

She writhes against me, arching her hips to greet my waiting cock. Her pussy's so wet and close, I could easily slip inside.

But not yet.

"Fallon, are you sure you want to do this?"

"I'm underneath you...*naked*," she counters, moving to give me more access to mark her neck.

"And you've been drinking," I argue. "I just have to know—"

"Levi, I want this as much as you."

Music to my fucking ears.

Standing, I move to my nightstand and pull out a condom. Then I hand it to her.

"Put this on me."

Fallon sits up and fumbles as she opens it. I almost offer to help, but then she slides the wrapper between her teeth and rips it. She looks at me mischievously as she slides it over my shaft.

Cupping her jaw, I tilt her mouth to meet mine and savor her sweet taste. Sour apple and cranberry cider mix with her natural taste, and it's a combo I'll never forget.

"Lie back, my love. Spread those legs for me."

Fallon scoots to the middle of the bed as I stroke myself, and then I kneel between her thighs.

"If you need me to stop for any reason, tap my shoulder twice. Got it?"

She nods, and I press a kiss to her lips before lining up with her entrance. Her breath hitches as soon as I push in, and my eyes roll back from how tight she is.

"Holy shit." She gasps when I thrust in all the way.

Inch by inch, I fill her deep and full.

"You feel so good, baby, and I've barely moved," I admit, then pull out slightly before slamming back in.

She leans up on her elbows and watches our bodies merge into one. I cup a hand around her neck and slightly pull her forward so she can get a better view.

"See how good we look together," I tell her before rotating my hips and pounding against her, over and over.

"God, yes." Her head falls back on her shoulders as I drive us toward the ledge, but I'm far from done with her.

"Play with your tits while I take care of this needy clit," I demand, pressing my thumb over her sensitive bud.

Fallon cups her breasts and tweaks her nipples tighter until her pussy's ready to explode.

"Shit, I think I'm close," she whimpers, rocking her hips faster. I squeeze harder and impale her on my shaft.

"Let go, sweetheart. Come on my cock."

With one hand between us and the other guiding her, she inhales sharply. Her eyes flutter, and her body stiffens.

"Levi, holy shit..." And then her pussy squeezes me with so much goddamn force, I have to use every ounce of strength to edge.

"Fucking hell, Fallon." I slow our rhythm and reach her mouth. "Tell me how many."

"*Two.*"

"Good girl. Now turn around and stick out that ass."

She obeys, getting on all fours and widening her legs. I cup her pussy from behind, feeling her sticky arousal between her folds before inserting two fingers. And just as I build her up for number three, I lower myself on the bed as far as I can and press my face between her ass cheeks.

"Levi, w-what are you doing..." Her rapid breathing as she releases harsh moans lets me know she doesn't hate it, so I keep going.

My tongue slides over her tight hole as my fingers return to her cunt, adding more pressure when I tickle her sensitive nub.

"I need you inside me, please," she begs, arching her back and spreading wider.

When I pull back, I replace my tongue with my thumb, and she gasps.

"I take it you've never experienced ass play, either?" I ask with amusement, though I know the answer. "Don't tense up. You'll enjoy it so much more if you relax."

"Does that go both ways?" she mocks. "Let me stick my fist in yours and see how you feel."

My palm smacks her backside, and I smile when her skin turns red. "So mouthy for someone who's about to get her brains fucked out. You'd think my tongue would've turned your grinchy attitude around."

"Stop talking about it and do it already."

I smirk at her greedy demand, allowing her to get used to my thumb. "Hold on tight. I'm about to fuck the Christmas spirit right into you."

As soon as my crown breaches her entrance, I slam inside as hard as I can. She nearly loses her balance, but I quickly wrap my arm around her waist and steady us.

"That better for you, Little Miss Seattle?" I whisper in her ear as I lean down.

She can barely breathe, let alone talk, so I take that as a yes.

Fallon's loud moaning has me teetering on the edge, desperate to explode and claim her as mine. But I want tonight to last as long as possible.

"You're so close. I can feel you shaking," I tell her, bringing my fingers around to her clit. "Back up into me and come, my love. Take what you need."

I keep still as she continuously slams herself on my cock, over and over until she's crying out my name. My fingers dig into her hips, and I wouldn't be surprised if bruises appear tomorrow.

"Fallon..." I warn when she collapses to the bed and flips onto her back.

"*Three,*" she finally breathes out.

I tower over her with my hands on either side of her and smirk when she wipes sweat from her forehead.

"Your pussy takes me so well." I dip down until my mouth clasps over her pebbled nipple.

"I might need to take a rain check on the other two."

I chuckle, feathering kisses between her breasts and sucking the soft skin above her collarbone.

"With the way your body responds and begs for more of me, we'll be surpassing five in no time," I say with amusement.

Her chest rises and falls, and I passionately kiss her, giving her time to regroup. When she takes my bottom lip in her mouth and tugs, I wrap an arm around her and flip us over until I'm on my back and she's straddling my waist. As I cup her face, I lean forward and slide my tongue between her swollen lips.

"Ride me like a good girl, and I'll reward you like a bad one. I want those tits bouncing in my face, baby."

"Don't forget you gave me permission to use anything you say in my article." She maneuvers down my legs and palms my aching cock, a dirty, sly smile on her gorgeous face.

"You have my permission to do whatever the hell you want," I tell her. "Give your boss a list of all the filthy ways I fucked you for all I care. That'd be one way to sell your magazine. Tourism would be at an all-time high."

Fallon's cheeks burn red as she tries not to laugh. "You're arrogant, you know that?"

"I think you mean the sweetest man you've ever met?" Then I smack her ass before adding, "Who has a dirty side."

She shifts until I'm back inside her, deep and tight, and I play with her greedy clit.

"That's it, my love. Now fuck me, Fallon."

And she does until her body loses control.

She throws her head back, screaming through her release.

"*Four*," she whispers without being prompted.

"You listen so nicely when you want to." I brush wild strands of hair off her forehead and bring her mouth to mine.

"I can't believe you're still hard."

Grinning, I teasingly thrust up into her. "I've been like this for the past three days, sweetheart."

"You're insatiable."

"I'm about to unleash inside you," I warn. "But I want you to turn around first."

She furrows her brow. "What?"

"Reverse cowgirl. I wanna see your ass while you ride me."

I can tell from her confused expression she doesn't know that position.

"Put your hands on my thighs for support and move like normal," I explain as she sits up. Once she's turned around, she snakes her legs underneath mine. I help guide her down my length, and we both let out a deep groan.

"Just like that." I lean up on one elbow as I use my other hand to grip a handful of her hair. "Let's come together, baby."

Fallon's sweet moans linger in the air as we race to the finish line. I could spend days being inside her like this.

"Fuck, you're so tight."

"I can't believe I'm about to..."

I tug on her hair just as the buildup between us takes over. When a shock of pleasure shoots through me, I groan. Fallon stiffens, and I know she's there, so I finally give myself permission to follow. I come with so much goddamn intensity that I swear I stop breathing for a solid minute.

"Holy shit." She rolls off my legs and collapses on the bed. "I'm numb."

Chuckling, I reach for her to lie next to me instead.

"I think you meant to say something else."

With an eye-roll and a smirk, she says, "*Five.*"

"And you took all of them like the badass you are." I lean over and press my lips to hers. "I'm going to shower. Do you want to join me?"

"I don't think I can."

I laugh, dragging up the crumpled blankets from the foot of the bed to cover her. "I'll bring you some water. Be right back."

After I pull on some sweats, I head downstairs and grab two bottles of water. My limbs are tight and sore as fuck already, but it was one thousand percent worth it.

The truth is, I've never had someone like Fallon.

She may not realize it, but she gives *me* a run for my money. Though I'm the one who sought to give her five orgasms, I've actually never done that before.

It was a first for me, too.

When I return, my bed's surprisingly empty.

"Fallon?"

"In the bathroom, hold on."

As soon as she reappears, I immediately recognize what she's wearing and am tempted as hell to rub my hands all over her again.

"Nice shirt." Grinning, I hand her one of the bottles, then gaze down my favorite heather-gray work shirt with our Christmas tree farm logo.

"Hope you don't mind. I'm not a fan of walking around naked like you." Her teasing tone has me breaking out into a smile.

"Really? 'Cause I'd be a big fan of you doing just that." Wrapping my arms around her waist, I pull her into my body, then inhale her skin's sweet smell.

"I bet you would be. Just like how you're a big fan of *snuggling*."

"Speaking of, are you gonna play your little game tonight of pretending to sleep in your bed before sneaking into mine and claiming it's because you're *so cold*? Don't get me wrong, I like this little back-and-forth, but I love it even more when you're next to me."

She playfully smacks my chest. "It's not my fault your furnace doesn't work."

"Yeah, what a bummer," I tease dryly.

"Wait...is it even broken? Did *you* pretend it was to get me into your bed?" She steps back, folding her arms over her chest as if she thinks she's onto something.

I pull her in closer. "No, I'm not that clever."

She gives me a side-eye. "I want to agree with you on that one, but I'm still suspicious."

I give her ass a playful tap, then walk backward toward the bathroom. "See you after my shower. Or at midnight...whenever you decide to join me."

DAY 7

Fallon wasn't in my room after my shower. She also didn't sneak into my bed in the middle of the night. I wasn't sure if she wanted me to go to her or be left alone, so I stayed in my room and waited.

A part of me is disappointed she never came. The other part of me knows she's leaving in a week, and it's probably best if we don't get too attached.

Though I have a feeling it's far too late for that.

Since it's Saturday and I have to work, I'll be leaving Fallon to do her own thing.

Dasher follows me downstairs, and I quickly refill his food and water dishes, then start some coffee and a cup of hot cocoa for myself.

As Dasher darts to the stairs, I see Fallon coming down. She looks like she got fucked into next week and back.

"Good morning." I smile as Dasher licks her.

"Not sure about that." She groans, wiping the slobber off the back of her hand. "I think that hard cider crept up on me."

I chuckle. "It tends to do that."

Though we both know the way she's feeling isn't just from the alcohol.

She sits on the stool and immediately puts her head down over her folded arms.

"Here, drink this." I slide a cup of hot coffee across the breakfast bar.

"Thanks." She lifts her head up long enough to blow on it, then takes a sip. "Mm. That's so good," she murmurs.

"I still don't know how you can drink it without milk or sugar."

She shrugs. "When you're constantly working like I am or on the road, you learn not to be a basic bitch, or you'll end up disappointed. At least plain coffee is nearly impossible to screw up unless, of course, it's instant."

"You were picky the day after you arrived, begging for caffeine."

"It was a long journey getting here. Give me a break."

Smirking, I lean against the counter. Her dark hair is pulled up on top of her head, and tangled strands frame her face. I wrap some behind her ear, taking in how gorgeous she is.

"I, uh..." She averts her gaze to the floor. Then she blinks before meeting my eyes. "We should probably talk about last night."

I check the time and decide I'd rather be late than wait all day for this discussion.

"Oh, if you've gotta go..."

"No, we can chat." I sit on the stool next to her and give her my undivided attention. By the expression on her face, I doubt her next words will be how mind-blowing last night was even though I know for a fact it was unlike anything either of us had experienced.

"First, I don't do that..." She waves her arm in the air. "Hookups or one-night stands. At least that's never my intention. But I want to be upfront and honest with you since we'll be in the same house for another week."

I scratch my cheek, definitely not liking where this conversation is headed.

"Sure, of course." I keep my expression indifferent, the same I use when I tell women a similar talk. I'm rarely ever on this side of the conversation, and I don't like it.

"What happened last night can't happen again. It was nice, but I'm here on business, and—"

"Nice? I'm sorry, but did you just say getting five orgasms was *nice*?

Puppies are nice. I think what we did last night goes a little above that threshold."

A blush forms over her cheeks before she purses her lips into a thin line again. "It was *very* nice, but regardless, it was still a mistake. We shouldn't have crossed the line when I'm leaving soon. I hope you can understand."

She looks genuinely sad, so I don't understand why she'd willingly waste the rest of our time together. But I don't fight her on it. Fallon's a grown woman, and I'll respect her decision.

"Sure, I get it. We just got caught up in the moment. It's fine."

"Really? You're not upset?"

"Fallon, what kind of guy do you think I am?" I press a fist to my chest, pretending to be wounded. Then I place a palm on her shoulder for reassurance. "If that's what you want, I'll act like it never happened, okay?"

"Just like that? Things won't be weird with me staying here?"

I rock my head back and forth with a grin. "Not any weirder than you showing up out of the blue and seeing me completely naked and spraying me with Mace."

Her shoulders drop. "Are you ever gonna let me live that down?"

Bellowing out a laugh, I shake my head. "*Never.*"

"So we're good?"

"Of course, Little Miss Seattle." I flash her a wink, then stand to find Dasher. "I'll be working most of the day, so help yourself to whatever. As if you need my permission."

"Ha ha. I'll probably drive into town and look around."

"Good, enjoy yourself and do some shopping. We're set to visit Bennett's Orchard Farm tomorrow, and then you're scheduled to meet with the mayor on Tuesday."

"Any updates from the furnace guy?" she asks, shivering.

"No, I suspect it'll be another few days. Don't worry, I'll chop some more wood so you don't freeze to death."

"Thanks. I appreciate that." She takes a large gulp of coffee. "You're not leaving me with Dasher again, are you?"

"No, I learned my lesson. He's coming to the farm with me." At the mention of his name, he trots over. "C'mon, boy. Time to go."

Dasher jumps up on Fallon and licks her face. "No, Dasher. Ew, stop it."

"Dasher, down." I snap my fingers, and he immediately obeys.

"How the hell do you do that?"

I wiggle my fingers at her. "It's all in the wrist, my love."

She rolls her eyes.

"Call or text if you need anything, okay?"

"Will do."

I grab my keys and wallet, then whistle for Dasher.

"Bye, Fallon," I call out as we head out the door.

"Bye."

And I walk out as if my heart isn't more bruised than it was this morning.

CHAPTER THIRTEEN

LEVI

DAY 8

I WORKED UNTIL DARK YESTERDAY, giving Fallon the space she needed. I kept myself busy and showed up with dinner like nothing had happened between us. She did the same, so now we're pretending that night doesn't exist.

"Ready?" I ask Fallon as we pull up to a rustic inn on Bennett's Orchard Farm.

"This place is like my second home," I explain as we climb out of the truck. We've had a strange energy between us all day that I can't seem to shake, but neither of us mentions it. Instead, I continue to act as if we didn't get lost together. It's easier than getting caught up in the emotions I'm not used to feeling.

So I tuck it away and act indifferent.

Fallon studies the inn for a moment, focusing on the white building with dark shutters.

"I spent many summers here helping," I say as Finn's younger cousin, Silas, walks toward us.

"This your girlfriend of the week?" he blurts out. He's tall with dark brown hair, and at a quick glance, he could be confused for Finn. But his smart mouth always gives him away.

Fallon gives him a weird look.

I clear my throat, interrupting the daggers she's shooting at him.

"Silas, this is Fallon Joy," I introduce, then explain what she's doing here.

"Ahh, a journalist. You know what they say about them?"

Fallon crosses her arms. "No, what do they say?"

"Nothing," I blurt out before Fallon can give Silas a verbal beating.

"Only that they're gorgeous," Silas tries saving his ass. "And from what I'm seeing, it's true."

Fallon's body relaxes, but she keeps her infamous scowl. "Are you a Christmas freak too?" Her gaze lands on his Christmas sweater peeking out of his unzipped jacket.

Silas's face breaks out into a grin, too damn happy to be getting her attention if you ask me.

"I can be any kind of freak you want, baby."

The fact that he is desperately trying to flirt with her, even though she's not taking the bait, has my jealousy rearing its ugly head.

"Oh perfect. I'm actually really into Daddy play," Fallon says in such a serious tone, I have to make sure I heard her correctly.

"Daddy *what*?" I scratch my head, still confused about whether she's messing with him.

"Oh, I could totally handle that," Silas blurts out, his eyes lowering down her body like a possession. "Call me Daddy anytime you want, princess."

"Alright…" I drawl, setting my palm against her lower back. "It's time to go."

I lead her toward the door, then glance over my shoulder at Silas.

"*Hot*," he mouths, and I shoot him a death glare.

"Sorry about him," I say once we're far enough away from him.

She snorts. "He seems harmless."

He is, but that doesn't mean I liked the way he looked at her.

Willa—my honorary grandma—comes from around the corner carrying a plate of apple turnovers. I snatch one, but it's so hot I have to pass it between my hands.

Willa laughs. "That's the risk you take when you snatch goodies from trays. These just came from the oven."

I blow on the pastry as Willa smiles at Fallon. "Hi. You must be Ms. Joy. We've been expecting you."

Fallon smiles sweetly. "Thank you for having me. I'm really happy to be here."

I take a bite, and the gooey apple filling burns the roof of my mouth. They both snicker as Willa offers Fallon a special tour of the inn.

"I'll survive," I offer. As they walk away, I take the opportunity to text Finn, letting him know we're on the property.

> **FINN**
> You still coming over this afternoon? I just got home and am jumping in the shower.

> **LEVI**
> Yep. Fallon's on her special tour. Be there right after.

> **FINN**
> Sounds good. See ya soon.

I check the time, and it's just past three. In the winter, he doesn't work long hours because it's the off-season. He also tries to spend as much time with Oakley as he can between her busy schedule.

After an hour, Fallon returns wearing a smile, and this one meets her eyes.

"Thank you again. I appreciate you taking the time to show me around and share the orchard's history. It's fascinating."

"You're welcome. I was serious about you visiting next year to experience our fall festival. You can stay here, my treat, but just let me know well in advance."

Fallon grins, but I notice how she doesn't immediately say yes.

"I'm sure it won't disappoint," she says.

"Would you like some pastries?"

"I wish I could, but I have to watch how much gluten I eat," she explains. "I'm sorry."

"Oh, I understand, sweetie. No worries."

"I guess we better get going. Finn and Oakley are expecting us."

Willa's eyes light up. "Please tell my grandson and my favorite new granddaughter I said hello."

"I will," I say, snagging an apple turnover for the road, then we make our way outside. The cool wind brushes against my cheeks, and I see Fallon shiver.

"That was fun," she admits as I open the passenger door of the truck so she can climb in. After I slide in the driver's side and crank the engine, I turn to her. "Are you still up for going to Finn and Oakley's house?"

"Yeah. Can't wait to meet them."

I try to keep the conversation going as we make our way across the property, but we don't talk about anything of substance.

"We won't stay too long," I tell her when we park.

She nods, and before we can knock, Oakley swings open the door and greets us.

"It's so nice to finally meet you, Fallon!"

Without thinking twice, Oakley pulls Fallon into a tight hug as if they're long-lost friends. At first, Fallon hesitates but then reciprocates. When they break apart, Oakley steps aside, allowing us in but turns to waggle her brows at me.

I smile and shake my head, not wanting her to play matchmaker.

Finn's sitting on the couch watching TV and immediately stands and introduces himself to her.

"I met your grandma earlier," Fallon explains.

"Oh, I bet that was an *experience.*"

"Very educational. She was sweet, though, and I learned a lot. Congrats on the centennial. I heard it was quite the event."

Although it was over a year ago, it's still the talk of the town.

"It was incredible," Oakley says. "I'd never experienced anything like it before."

"Yeah, Levi told me," Fallon says. "I saw your painting in the town hall and the one you did for the tree farm. Your talent is amazing."

Oakley blushes. "Thank you. I'm glad you liked them."

"I could've stared at that fall festival painting for hours."

With a laugh, Oakley turns to me. "Okay, I like her."

"I haven't met anyone who hasn't," I say truthfully, meeting Fallon's beautiful eyes. A silent conversation streams between us before Oakley speaks up.

"Want to see some small things I'm working on?" Oakley asks, and Fallon immediately agrees. They move to the far side of Finn's place, and I'm grateful for Oakley's ability to keep the conversation flowing. She's really great at making anyone feel comfortable.

"Would you guys like some *adult* eggnog?" Finn asks.

I follow him into the kitchen as he pulls everything from his fridge, along with the amaretto and rum.

As the girls are busy talking, Finn sets out four glasses, then stares up at me. "You fucked her, didn't you?"

I narrow my eyes, trying my best not to give myself away. "Don't know what you're talking about."

He furrows his brow as if he's waiting for me to break, and I eventually do. "It's not like that." It wasn't just a one-night stand for me even though that's ultimately what it turned into.

Finn laughs. "That's what they all say."

"She's different," I mutter, keeping my voice low while stealing a glance over at the girls.

"Wait, you actually *like-like* her."

"Shut up," I say, not wanting them to overhear.

"C'mon, spill the beans."

I lean my lower back against the counter, watching Fallon as Finn mixes our drinks. "Something happened between us that she's made clear she doesn't want to happen again."

"Ah, I see. The tables have turned, and you're finally doing the chasing."

"I'm not *chasing* anyone," I argue. "That hasn't changed."

"It will. I basically said the same thing. It's what we like to call denial, especially when we meet *the one.*"

I glare at him.

"Whatever. You're too stubborn to admit shit, I get it. Good luck because you'll need it when it's time for her to go. Letting her leave will be the hardest thing you've ever done. Take it from someone who experienced that kind of heartache."

"Yeah, I remember…" He was a goddamn mess. Luckily, Oakley returned two weeks later to put him out of his misery.

He hands me my glass, then delivers the others to the girls.

Fallon will only be here for another week, and I'll keep her at arm's length until she leaves because that's what she wants.

As if she knows I'm thinking about her, she meets my eyes from across the room, then takes a sip. Her gaze lingers a little too long, and I break the spell by looking away. I swallow hard, not wanting to think about what she stirs inside me, replaying the words she said the next morning.

Finn returns and grabs his eggnog. "Everything okay?"

"Yeah," I say, following him to the living room. Fallon and I sit on the couch, our arms brushing as we get comfortable.

After Finn sits in the armchair, Oakley takes his lap.

"So we have some news," Finn says.

"We're engaged!" Oakley quickly announces before I can even guess.

"I proposed last week, but we wanted to tell you in person," Finn explains.

"Congrats!" I stand to give Oakley and Finn each a hug. We're all smiles as Oakley explains exactly how it all happened. It's impossible not to notice how they look at each other with intense love and admiration.

After we've finished our first round of spiked eggnog, Finn gives us refills.

"I guess it's time to tell all the embarrassing stories about Levi," Finn taunts when he returns with fresh drinks.

"Oh, yes please," Fallon quips. "Though I have a couple of my own already."

I shake my head. "Bad idea."

"*Perfect* idea," Oakley counters.

"So there was this one time when Levi's parents went out of town for a day right around Christmas—"

I quickly interrupt him. "Come on, man. You don't have to tell this one."

Based on the look he gives me, the rum is already making its way through his system.

"Anyway, Levi asked if I wanted to come over after school, so I did."

Oakley snickers like she's heard this story before.

I narrow my eyes at her, silently warning her to stop engaging.

"What?" She shrugs. "I know how this ends."

Fallon eagerly waits for him to tell the rest.

"So I have my mom drop me off, and what does Levi do? He makes me keep watch for his parents as he meticulously opens several gifts under the tree. He was so good at it, too. He'd slip the boxes back in the same paper, and you couldn't even tell they'd been touched."

"Wait, how old were you?" Fallon asks me.

"Twelve."

She smirks. "So…old enough to know better."

"Oh yeah," Finn agrees. "Anyway, he's in the living room playing this game when his parents drive up. When his mom walks into the living room and sees the box on the table and the toy in Levi's hand, she nearly loses her shit."

"Oh no." Fallon laughs.

"Levi tries to lie his way out of it, but Mrs. White doesn't take the bait. She demanded he donate all his gifts to charity so he'd learn a lesson."

Fallon's eyes widen. "Ouch."

I sigh. "Trust me when I say I have never been able to live it down. All these years later, Lucy brings it up anytime she can."

"Speaking of Lucy, she's the one who snitched so their mom would come home early."

"Wow, she plays dirty." Fallon chuckles.

"We're twins…it's not fun without a little pranking. To be honest, I deserved it. I read her online diary and then told all her crushes what she wrote about them."

"Oh my God." Fallon's jaw drops. "That's evil."

I shrug. "We were kids!"

We're laughing our asses off, and when Fallon leans into me, I feel her body heat and smell her shampoo. I'm tempted to wrap my arm around her and pull her closer.

"That kind of reminds me of something that happened to my older sister when I was a kid. But to make matters worse, she had snuck her boyfriend over instead of her best friend," Fallon says with a grin. "There was another time my mom caught them making out on her bed. After that, there was a strict open-door policy, and no boys allowed in our rooms.

You'd think they were having sex or something by the way my mom acted, but they weren't."

"Oh man. I bet that was embarrassing for her," Oakley says.

"It's okay, though. My sister actually married that boy, so it all worked out."

"I bet your mom had countless stories to tell at the wedding," Oakley says.

Fallon gives a small smile that doesn't quite meet her eyes. "Unfortunately, no. She passed away before she got the chance to do that."

Awkwardness fills the room, and Oakley apologizes profusely. I'm angry with myself for not knowing this and somewhat hurt that she didn't tell me. Not that she owes me details about her life, but she already knows so much about me and my life.

"I'm so sorry," I offer.

Fallon shakes her head. "No, it's okay. I forgot for a moment that you guys don't know about my past. I'm so used to everyone knowing, and I just got lost in the moment." She pauses for a moment. "Guess my sister is right. I really am the grinch and am apparently *really* great at ruining good times. Please forgive me." Fallon sets her half-full glass on the coffee table and smiles.

"You're not a grinch," Oakley speaks up, quickly changing the subject. I'm appreciative of how intuitive she is. "Now this guy, he was the grinchiest grinch I'd ever met."

Finn furrows his brow. "Am not."

"Bullshit. You still are sometimes. Get this…" Oakley says. "When I first arrived, he was so damn rude. Didn't even introduce himself! He picked me up from the airport, and it was an hour of pure awkward silence."

"That must've been uncomfortable as hell."

"It was *painful*," Oakley admits, laughing at Finn.

"Okay, I think you might actually have me beat," Fallon concedes.

"Pfft. You literally pepper sprayed me in my own house," I argue. "I think you might win this one."

Fallon beams. "And you were naked."

"It was my *bedroom*," I remind her, though she doesn't need it.

"Imagine a strange naked man walking toward you in a place you thought you just rented. I thought he was there to murder me! What would you do?"

"I don't blame you one bit," Oakley agrees. "Too bad I didn't have any Mace on hand when I met you," she directs to Finn.

"For what? I let you stay in my house—sleep in my bed, rather,—and I drove your ass around," Finn reminds her, and Fallon and I laugh.

"Yes, but you were grumpy about it the whole time."

"Well…" I grin. "Not the *whole* time. You two were pretty handsy."

"I eventually won him over." Oakley beams.

Finn turns to Fallon. "Have you tasted his famous gingersnap cookies yet?"

"The ones at the shop?" Fallon asks.

"Yep, those are the ones," Finn confirms. "But no one knows how to make them. The top secret recipe has been in their family for seven generations. You basically have to be a White or marry one. Apparently being his childhood best friend wasn't even enough to get it."

Fallon snorts.

"My grandma's tried to recreate it, but no one can figure out how to make them just right. If you do, I'll pay top dollar," Finn tells her.

"It's actually *eight* generations," I muse.

"Just spill it already. I won't tell a soul."

"What's so secret about it?" Fallon asks, glancing back and forth between us.

"If I told ya, I'd have to marry ya." I shoot her a wink.

Fallon gives me a mischievous grin. "I thought you were allergic to the M word."

Finn and Oakley bellow out in laughter.

"Nah, still searching for the right one who can handle me," I state, hoping she gets the hint.

"Well, good luck finding her," Fallon mocks.

"Oh, you'll settle down eventually. You're just a big ole cinnamon roll, and eventually, you'll find your Cinnabon," Oakley tells me.

"Thanks for believing in me," I say with a laugh.

Oakley and Finn carry the glasses to the kitchen, and Fallon bumps her body against mine. "Cinnamon roll, huh?"

I give her a smile. "Are you really surprised?"

"That must explain why you're so warm on the outside and gooey on the inside."

I wish I could place my fingers at the bottom of her chin and kiss the fire out of her. Our eyes stay locked as she licks her bottom lip. For a few seconds, everything around us disappears, and I watch her eyes flutter closed. Before I can lean in to kiss her, Oakley walks over with a six-pack of hard cider.

"Wanted to give this to you since it's your favorite," she explains.

I grab it, and when Fallon looks at which flavor it is, Oakley mouths, "Sorry," realizing she interrupted a moment. I give a slight shake of my head, then check the time, knowing we need to get going.

As we stand to say our goodbyes, I congratulate my friends again on their engagement, then drive us home.

"I like them a lot," Fallon admits, and it makes my heart happy to hear that. I can almost imagine her staying here forever. Even if it's wishful thinking, the thought makes me smile.

CHAPTER FOURTEEN

FALLON

DAY 10

I TYPE AWAY on my laptop and sip my coffee between my thoughts.

Yesterday, while Levi was at work, I drove into town and met the mayor. He took it upon himself to give me a personal tour of the town, picking up right where Levi left off.

To be honest, it was hard to take him seriously when he was dressed like Santa Claus. He was in good spirits and sang *ho, ho, ho* to each child that walked past. I tried to smile when I was supposed to, knowing how much my mother would've loved this place.

It's amazing to see so many welcoming of his presence. If the previous mayor of Seattle walked into my office at work, I'd have some choice words. This community really does act like a big family, even when Levi isn't around.

I can't count how many times people have asked about me staying at Levi's. News really does spread fast in small towns.

As I continue typing, I'll randomly glance at all the notes I took on my phone. Even though that was yesterday, my brain is still full and overwhelmed. My fingers fly across the keyboard, the sentences pouring out of me like water. I'm trying my best to stay professional and keep my personal bias out of my prose. However, it's hard at times.

Before I start my next paragraph, there's a knock on the door. Dasher lifts his head but doesn't get up. Levi was going to take him with him today, but I actually asked if he could stay with me. He was shocked at first, but I didn't want to be alone.

I see an old work truck outside and open the door.

"Hey, I'm Jasper. Here to fix the furnace."

"Yeah, Levi told me you were stopping by." Stepping aside, I allow him to walk in. He's carrying a toolbox in one hand and a clipboard in the other, reminding me of my dad.

"Do you know where you need to go?" I ask.

"Yes, I do. Thanks," he says and makes his way to the utility closet.

I return to the couch and get settled, rereading what I wrote before I stopped. Dasher repositions himself and plops back down. I add a few more words but then get distracted by an incoming email. It's my travel itinerary for my January assignment.

I'll be writing an article about small coffee roasters in Washington, which I'm actually looking forward to. Can't wait to drink my weight in dark roasts.

When I see I'm staying at a well-known hotel chain, I let out a sigh of relief. Not sure I could survive this rental mix-up again, even if it ended up working out.

After an hour, Jasper returns and tells me it's finally fixed. He adjusts the thermostat, and the heat immediately kicks on. I scrunch my nose when the smell of burning oil surfaces.

"That's normal since it hasn't run in a while. It'll go away," he reassures me.

"Thank you so much," I say as I follow him to the door.

"Tell Levi I'll bill him," he says, then waves.

"Sure will."

When he's gone, Dasher rushes past me before I can close the door. Quickly, he goes outside, does his business, and then returns.

I look at him with my jaw on the floor. "Seriously?"

I swear, I can't figure this dog out.

After I lock the deadbolt, I feed Dasher a few treats, and then make myself some soup. As I sit down to eat, I hear my phone buzzing in the living room and rush to grab it.

"Sis!" Taryn says, laughing. "I sent the picture of that guy you're staying with to my mom-friends group chat, and they want more."

"How did you get a picture of him?"

"I looked up the Christmas tree farm on Instagram and sleuthed around until I saw his name. Levi White. I'd let him play lumberjack and climb me like a tree."

I groan. "He doesn't *climb* them. He chops them down."

"Well, whatever. But I need you to give me all the details because my friends are highly invested."

"There's nothing to share."

"Why do I suspect you're not telling me the truth? Let that man eat you like a candy cane. We've all been living vicariously through all the scenarios we've made up about you two. We've even started a pool of money."

"For what?" If only she could see my face.

"For when you two finally become a couple."

"That's not happening."

"But it'd be cool if it did," she says. "Imagine your beautiful children. My future niece or nephew would be gorgeous. Big green eyes with dark hair. I'm picturing it now."

"You're ridiculous. And a little weird."

"Maybe a little. So how's the writing going?"

"Okay, I guess. I did a lot this morning. Now I'm eating," I tell her, settling back at the breakfast bar. I catch her up, explaining the nuances of this town and the things I find interesting.

When our conversation comes to a lull, I change the subject. "Have you talked to Dad lately?"

"A few days ago," she tells me. "He was doing okay. Why?"

"I was just thinking about him."

"Should give him a call," she suggests.

"Yeah, maybe I will," I offer. "How are my favorite nieces?"

"They've been extra good, but that's what happens when Christmas is in less than two weeks. All I have to do is mention the naughty list or that god-forsaken elf, and the fighting stops. I'm going to be sad when I can't use that to my advantage anymore." She laughs.

They're the perfect little family, and while I never try to compare myself, my sister makes me feel like I'm being left behind in the game of getting married and having a family. It's great being independent and doing what I love, but I still wish I had more purpose in my life.

She continues on as I finish my soup, and when she gets another call, we say our goodbyes. Dasher lazes by my feet. Instead of moving back to the living room, I decide to stay and work from here.

There's a perfect view of the pond, and now that the furnace is working, the entire house is toasty warm. As I stare out the window, letting my mind wander, I decide to finally call my dad. It rings a few times, and I almost expect him not to answer, but he does.

"Hey, honey. Happy holidays."

I scoff. "Bah Humbug."

"Somehow I knew you'd say that. How have things been going?"

We'd briefly chatted before my trip here, so I fill him in on the latest but leave out the parts that would make him worry.

"Everyone is very nice here. The town really is like the North Pole," I explain. "And the mayor dresses like Santa and hands out candy canes."

Dad chuckles. "That sounds like your own personal hell."

"Oh, it is," I admit. "But it's not as bad as I thought it'd be. Or I'm just warming up to it now."

"That's good, at least. Maybe you'll find the Christmas spirit while you're there." He muffles like he's holding back laughter.

"Yeah, yeah." I swallow hard, thinking about what Levi said about *Christmas spirit* the night we slept together. I ask about my stepmom, Shannon, and I can hear the smile in his voice when he talks about her.

"She's great now that I let her decorate the house for the holidays. Honestly, I'm still getting used to it."

My dad met Shannon while I was in college eight years ago, and they hit it off immediately. I don't have a relationship with her, but she's always been kind. Plus, my father seems happy, and that's really all I want for him.

"Yeah, I understand that," I say, scanning Levi's house. My mom was the only other person I knew who loved Christmas as much as him.

"Well, sweetheart, I should probably let you get back to your writing. Keep in touch, okay?"

"I will. Love you, Dad."

"Love you too, my little grinch."

Laughter escapes me as I end the call, feeling much better now that I've heard his voice. This time of year is always the hardest for me, and I usually dive into work without a second thought. My sister has her family and my dad has Shannon, and then there's me, the scrooge who refuses to celebrate. Before they take hold and ruin the rest of my day, I push those thoughts away.

Wanting a mindless task, I scroll through my social media feeds. Eventually, I pull myself away, then work for another hour before I realize my bladder is about to explode. I get up and rush to the bathroom. When I return, the back door opens and closes, and I smile, knowing Levi's finally home.

I hate to admit it, but I miss him when he's gone.

"Hi," I say, keeping my tone flat.

"Damn, it's hot in here. Guess Jasper stopped by?" He strips off his gloves, jacket, and hat.

"Yep, around lunch. It's a perfect seventy-five degrees," I say, returning to my stool.

He adjusts the temperature, and I turn, huffing at him. "Hey! I'm making up for lost heat."

"Woman, my balls are sweating. I know that's too much information, but I can't breathe in this heat. It feels like I'm suffocating. I'll have to walk around naked, and you've already warned me against doing that."

I hold back laughter. "Fine."

Dasher gets up and Levi lets him out. I put in my earbuds and turn on some calming sounds.

My fingers fly over the keys. I do everything I can to smack down my inner editor and move forward. As I'm writing about the mayor, I feel Levi hovering.

I take my earbud out and slightly close my screen, then glare at him. "What are you doing?"

"You can't publish that."

My face transforms into the dirtiest look I can manage. "Excuse me?"

"It's too bland. Are you writing a history piece or an article about a Christmas town?"

This pisses me off. "I didn't realize *you* were an expert. Why should I listen to you?"

He laughs, which only annoys me further. "It's lacking the feel of the town. No magic is pouring from the pages."

"Well, maybe that's because I haven't felt anything remotely magical."

"Liar."

"The people I've met have been kind and helpful. My integrity is on the line, and above anything, I'm honest. Maybe it doesn't have *magic*, but this is my first draft, and I haven't self-edited yet. Maybe my opinion will change after the festival, but right now, I don't see how it's any different from any other wintery ski town I've been to."

"That's it."

My brows crease.

"Guess I'm gonna have to bring it up a notch then."

"What does that even mean?"

"You'll see. When do you leave again?"

"Sunday, the day after the festival." I've already been here for ten days, and it's crazy to think I only have four left.

He rubs his palms together, then pulls his phone from his pocket. "Guess I better get to work then."

"Explain."

He flashes a shit-eating smirk that I don't like. "You'll see, Little Miss Seattle. You'll see."

CHAPTER FIFTEEN

LEVI

DAY 11

"You're sure about this?" Fallon asks as we pull up to the shop at the Christmas tree farm. Dasher sits between us and stares out the window. I put on his snow shoes and jacket this morning because we'll be outside most of the day.

"I've never been more serious about anything in my life." I shoot her a wink, and she playfully rolls her eyes. "You're going to have fun helping my sister. Hopefully not too much fun, though. No gossiping."

Fallon lifts a brow. "Oh, there will definitely be. Hope I don't screw up the wrapping though or make a kid cry."

I chuckle, looking at the parking lot that's full. "You said you wanted the full experience, so today, you're getting it."

"Well I'm up for the challenge," she states, and I wonder if she realizes she's been my biggest challenge to figure out.

I tell Dasher to stay and leave the truck running for him so he can enjoy the heat.

Inside the shop is complete chaos. The line of people buying last-minute wooden carved gifts is out the door. Mom gives me a quick wave as Fallon follows me to the gift-wrapping station.

After we make it through the crowd, I find Lucy wearing a candy cane apron with scissors, tape, and ribbon stuffed in the front pockets.

"There's the woman of the hour," she says as soon as Fallon comes into sight.

"Please don't give her a hard time," I warn, and Lucy snorts.

"We'll be besties by the end of the day." Lucy grins, wrapping her arm around Fallon, and then leading her behind the long table.

Fallon turns and looks at me like a deer in the headlights.

"I'll be back to pick you up after lunch, so try to survive until then."

"We'll take good care of her," Lucy says, waving me away.

Fallon's face cracks into a smile, and I know she'll do just fine, even if Lucy forces her to wear an apron just like hers.

"Watch those two, please?" I tell my mom as I walk past the counter and out the door.

Dasher wags his tail when he sees me, and I pet his head when I get in.

"Ready for our adventure?"

He tries to lick me as I put the truck in drive. I head across the property toward one of the barns where the horses are kept for the sleigh rides. It's been something the farm has done for over a century, and our patrons enjoy it.

As I walk into the barn with Dasher trotting beside me, I find Darrell brushing one of the horses. He's worked here for over a decade and knows his way around the farm.

"Hey, Levi. How's it going?" He secures a blanket on one of the horses. When the season cools, we make sure to put these on the animals to help regulate their temperature.

"No complaints. I'm alive and well," I say truthfully.

He gives me a nod. "Good to hear. What can I help you with?"

"I was thinking about taking Fallon on a sleigh ride."

"It's a perfect day for that. I can get the horses ready, if you'd like."

"That would be amazing. I have a few things I need to take care of first, but I'd just need them ready for right after lunch."

"Will do."

I thank him before heading back to my truck. Dasher hops in, and then we make my way across the property. Since the countdown to Christmas has officially begun, I drive to the loading dock and offer an extra hand.

All day long, these guys are wrapping, loading, and tying trees up for our customers.

A line of vehicles waits when I arrive. Dasher follows me around as I help lift and strap down trees to roofs. It's nonstop, and many are thankful for the extra help.

"Honestly, I didn't think it would be this busy today," Samuel, one of our seasonal helpers, admits. It's his first year working on the farm, so he's not fully accustomed.

I laugh. "Oh, just wait until next week. This is nothing."

His eyes are as wide as saucers. "You're kidding, right?"

I give him a hard pat on the back. "Not at all. You get used to it, though."

Once the crowd finally clears, I check my watch, then decide to leave now that they're in a better place. I head straight home to get everything ready for my surprise. As soon as I walk inside, my phone buzzes in my pocket. I expect to see a text asking me to come back and help. However, it's Finn.

> **FINN**
> How are things going? Have you proposed yet?

> **LEVI**
> Ha. Ha. Ha.

> **FINN**
> Oh, don't be like that. You know you like her.

> **LEVI**
> Can't have feelings for someone who will never reciprocate them.

> **FINN**
> Yeah, I can understand that. But I saw the sparks flying between you two. And so did Oakley.

> **LEVI**
> Then I guess you're both delusional.

FINN

Whatever you say. Anyway, we should get
together soon and grab a beer.

LEVI

Yeah, that sounds like a plan but after Christmas.

FINN

Sounds good. Have fun with your girlfriend.

LEVI

I send him two middle-finger emojis and then lock my phone. After
I've fed Dasher, I pull two large thermoses from the cabinet and prepare
my favorite hot chocolate recipe. I grab the small bottle of Irish liquor that
I keep in my fridge and put it in a bag.

I make sure to pack the heating blanket I borrowed from my mom and
grab the portable power tank from my shed. After I've double-checked
that I've got everything, I shoot my sister a text and let her know I'm on
my way there.

LUCY

Your timing is impeccable. We just finished eating.

LEVI

Perfect.

I look at Dasher. "Wanna go on a sleigh ride?"

His tail wags.

"I didn't hear you? Sleigh ride?" I ask again.

He barks several times. "Okay, let's go impress Little Miss Seattle."

Before we make our way to the gift shop, I park at the barn. When I get
out, I see Darrell has secured the harnesses on the horses. I go inside to let
him know we're here, and he helps me hook them to the sleigh. Dasher
jumps onto the front bench seat, and I load everything I brought for our
trip.

"This for a date?" Darrell asks with a knowing grin.

I shrug, not wanting to say either way.

He lifts a brow and nods as if he knows better.

"Thanks for everything. Probably be back in a couple of hours." I step up, plug in the heating blanket, and set our thermoses in the cup holders.

"Sounds good. I'll be here," he says.

I wave, then grab the reins, and we take off.

The horses jolt forward, the sleigh sliding across the blanket of white as Dasher sits upright next to me, looking around for rabbits. I pet him as we continue forward.

When I see the gift shop in the distance, I text my sister, letting her know I'm close. Five minutes later, I come to a halt beside the building and Fallon walks out. Her eyes meet mine and I smile, but she looks shocked.

"Hop on," I say, patting the seat next to me.

She glances at the horses and then meets my gaze again. "You went through all this trouble for me?"

"Trouble?" I chuckle. "It was nothing."

When Fallon comes close, I stand, offering her my hand. She takes it, then steps up, and I pull with a little too much force, causing her to crash into me.

"Sorry," I say, our faces mere inches apart.

She's breathless.

As she sits, I grab the blanket and place it on her legs.

Her mouth falls open. "Oh my God. It's so warm."

"Couldn't have you freezing out here." I settle down beside her. "Having portable battery tanks has been a game changer."

She glances back at it and smiles. "Thank you. This is already perfect."

As people start to crowd around the horses, I take that as my cue to leave. "You ready?"

She nods with enthusiasm as I guide the horses behind the gift shop and away from the people.

Once we're on the trail, I hand her a thermos. "Hot cocoa. And be careful. It's *very* hot."

She unscrews the top with her gloved hand and steam rises from inside. "Mm. Smells amazing."

Reaching down, I pick up and hand her the bottle of Irish cream liquor. "In case you'd like to add some spice."

Her brow pops up. "Don't mind if I do."

Fallon pours several shots inside, then takes a sip. When she moans, I silently convince my cock to calm down.

"It's the perfect temperature now." She looks down at my thermos. "Want me to add some to yours?"

"Sure."

Fallon pours it until the liquid touches the top.

"You tryin' to get me drunk?" I tease.

"Would it be the worst thing to happen?"

"Considering I'm the only one of us who knows how to get us back to the barn…"

"Okay, you actually have a point there. I'll trade you since I had a heavy hand." She drinks mine and laughs.

Fallon's eyes trail over our surroundings, and she relaxes.

"Where are you taking me? To your murder cabin?" She snorts.

"Yep." I laugh.

She bumps her body into mine but doesn't pull away. I welcome the closeness.

"I thought I'd take you to one of my favorite spots to visit during the winter."

"Oh, awesome."

"Can't wait for you to see it." We climb up a hill, then race down the other side.

Fallon shivers, so I pull the blanket up higher around her shoulders and rest my arm around her. "For more warmth," I whisper in a hushed tone.

"You're my own personal human heater," she says, and I give her a smirk, wishing that were still true. She hasn't been in my bed since we crossed the line.

Fallon laughs, and I glance over at her.

"I just realized that the sleigh bells on the horses aren't getting on my nerves. Usually they would."

This comes out of left field but has me grinning. "Really? It no longer sounds like nails on a chalkboard?"

"Maybe I'm becoming immune. I almost like it combined with the horses' hooves trotting along the snow," she admits. "It's kind of relaxing."

"Color me shocked," I taunt. "Next thing I know, you'll be singing carols."

She shakes her head. "Don't hold your breath on that one."

A cool breeze blows through the trees, and white powder kicks up in front of us. As we turn the corner, the scene is revealed, and Fallon gasps.

I bring the horses to a stop so she can take it in.

"It's beautiful," Fallon whispers, looking at the large frozen pond, snow-covered hills, and massive evergreens dusted in white. We stay silent as we listen to the sounds of our breathing and the wind whistling through the trees.

She pulls out her phone and snaps a picture. "I don't want to forget this moment."

"Me neither." But it's not because of the landscape.

When she smiles at me, the happiness actually reaches her eyes. "You know what I've always wanted to do?"

I search her face. "What?"

"Make a snow angel."

I chuckle. "Then that's what we have to do. Right now."

Dasher hops down and runs through the snow, enjoying himself, and I tie the horses to a nearby tree. I meet Fallon on her side of the sleigh and hold out my hand. She takes it and nearly stumbles as she steps down, but I catch her.

"So there's a trick to making the perfect one. You hold your hands out like this in a T, then you fall back just like this," I say, doing it. "Then you move your arms like you're doing jumping jacks. The trick is taking your time to stand so you don't disturb it."

Fallon chuckles as I make my creation, then I slowly stand.

"You were right! It *is* perfect," she tells me.

"As if you doubted me," I say, leading her over to some undisturbed snow. "We'll do this one together."

I take a step away from her, creating enough space so she'll be able to move her arms and legs. "Ready?"

She nods.

"Three. Two. One," I count down, and we fall backward. Fallon giggles as she thrashes in it.

"It's so cold!" She squeals, repeating what I told her to do, then we stand. "Look."

"I think these are the two best damn snow angels I've ever seen."

She laughs and nods while she takes a picture with her phone. After she snaps it, it slips from her grip. Fallon goes to retrieve it, but when she straightens back up, snow slams into me.

My jaw drops at seeing her up-to-no-good face.

"That's war," I warn, quickly packing a ball and launching it back at her. The next thing I know, we're running around like teenagers, making snowballs, chunking them across the way and laughing as we try to hit the other. Dasher barks while chasing us around, and I smile so much my face hurts.

Fallon races toward me, stumbles forward, and trips me. I hold her, bracing her fall as we land in the snow.

"I thought you'd be harder to take down than that," she teases.

"That's because you're a force to be reckoned with."

She smiles, and for a moment, I see something flash behind her eyes. She licks her lips and studies my mouth, and I'm tempted to kiss her. Unsaid emotions stream between us, pulling us closer. The anticipation of having her tongue slide against mine again is almost too much. Her eyes flutter closed, and I slowly move forward. Right before our lips crash together, Dasher plows into Fallon, and she falls to her side as he keeps playing. Fallon throws snow in his direction and he barks at it, trying to catch it in his mouth.

"Dasher," I groan, hating that he ruined the moment but also finding it hilarious.

Once both of Fallon's feet are firmly planted on the ground, she offers to help me up. As I stretch out my hand, I simultaneously reach behind me and grab another fistful of snow. She doesn't realize it until it crashes into her forehead.

Fallon growls, then the fight continues until we're breathless. Dasher is having the time of his life out here, and I'm almost willing to bet Fallon is too.

After admiring the view a little longer, we make our way back to the sleigh, and then ride toward the barn.

"You know, I don't think I've enjoyed myself this much during the holidays since before my mom died," Fallon admits as we sit close together.

"Really?"

She nods, and I can see she's lost in her head.

"I'm honored, Fallon. Do you want to talk about it?"

She sucks in a deep breath and unscrews the top of the hot cocoa, taking a big swig. "My mom passed away two days after Christmas. The anniversary is something I dread every year." She pauses. "You know, I hear these stories about people with sick parents who had time to prepare themselves for the worst. I didn't get that because my mom was gone in a blink."

"I'm sorry," I offer. "I know it's cliché, and that's probably what everyone says, but no one should ever lose a parent at a young age."

"I appreciate it. I was eleven when she passed. Taryn's two years older and helped me a lot, but it wasn't her responsibility to raise me. My teen years were difficult without my mom. We were all grieving at the same time too, which didn't help."

"I can't imagine, but I can understand why you wouldn't like this time of year. I'd feel the same way."

"Thanks," she whispers, and I place my arm around her back, offering what comfort I can.

"I live with a lot of guilt that she died."

I look over at her. "How come?"

"My mom would do anything for us girls, and that night, we wanted McDonald's. Mom didn't care that it was raining. Living in Seattle, you learn to deal and drive in it. On her way there, a drunk driver swerved into her lane and crashed into her. She died instantly."

I pull her closer into me. Instinctively, I rub her arm, then place a soft kiss on her forehead. "That's not your fault, sweetheart. You don't have to live with that on your conscience. Your mom obviously loved you and wanted to make you happy."

She wipes a few tears away, and it breaks my fucking heart.

"The day my mom died was the day Christmas became dead to me. I buried every ounce of holiday spirit I had with my mom because it was her favorite holiday. She used to go all out with decorating, and we had a light-viewing tradition. There would be trees in every room, advent calendars leading up to Christmas Day. She did everything in her power to make it special for us. Being here with you made me remember things I've kept buried for a long time. The happy times with my mom are nice memories to have, and I'll forever be grateful for that."

I give her a sweet smile. "Guess that scammer didn't ruin everything after all."

She snorts. "I know I've completely taken over your space and have gotten in your way."

In my heart too, but I don't say that. "I've enjoyed having you around. It's made me realize a lot of things. Plus, Dasher loves his new babysitter." I reach over and pet his head. For the past few days, something intense has been brewing between us, and I'm convinced she feels it too.

She looks over at Dasher. "He's still a little shit even though he's cute."

"Yeah, but ya like him. Just admit it already," I tease. Wishing we had the courage to put our hearts on the line.

CHAPTER SIXTEEN

FALLON

WE CONTINUE DOWN THE TRAIL, jingle bells jangling, and I feel as if the elephant that's been sitting on my back for the past twenty years has moved over a little.

"What are you thinking about?" Levi asks before I get too lost in my head.

"I've never shared that about my mom with anyone outside of my sister and dad," I admit.

"How come?"

I shrug. "I guess it just seemed like a lot of emotional baggage to throw on someone. It's always an awkward thing to bring up, and people usually don't know what to say or how to act. So I keep it to myself. Plus it's always been so hard for me to articulate how I've felt over the years."

"That makes sense."

"Once my mom was gone and my sister moved out, my dad fell into depression and so did I. Neither of us talked about it, and I guess we thought that if we ignored it, it'd disappear. The holidays were always a reminder of what we lost. I asked him if we could stop celebrating because it was too painful, so we pretended it didn't exist. We should've gone to therapy, but my dad is very stubborn when it comes to talking about his emotions or problems."

"Sounds like you two have a lot in common," Levi says with soft eyes, and I smile.

"I'm more like my dad than I like to admit sometimes. My sister is just like my mom."

"I know you don't need rescuing, Fallon, but damn I would if you'd let me."

My heart flutters, and I don't know what to say. I touch the necklace around my neck, and he smiles. "My mom's."

He nods. "I figured it was."

"I never take it off," I tell him. "I'm always scared that if I do, I'll lose it. My sister has one too and hasn't taken it off since the day she got it."

"So you don't have to answer this question if you don't want to, but has your sister canceled Christmas as well?"

I slowly exhale. "No, she has kids and loves Christmas as much as our mom did. While it took a lot for her to get there, she eventually came around. Her husband really helped her through everything. My dad eventually remarried when I was twenty-two, and my stepmom pulled him out of his shell, too. Then there's me. The single Scrooge."

"I can think of a few other names to add to that list," he teases.

I laugh as snow falls on my eyelashes. "Scrooge. Grinch. Christmas Karen. I've been called them all over the years. But I guess if the name fits. I'm the only one who's stuck living in the past."

"I was going to say kind, beautiful, inspiring, strong . You're not a hater because the happiness of it annoys you, it goes deeper than that, and I understand now. I'm sorry if I'm over the top."

"Don't apologize for being yourself, Levi. You've made me see things differently. Out of all the places in town, the scammers sent me to Mr. Holly Jolly's house. Ironic, right?"

He chuckles. "It is, but I've been saying that since the beginning."

"Do you think it's divine intervention or something?" I ask, as snow flurries surround us. The horses' hooves kick up the snow. Dasher doesn't seem fazed as he looks around.

"Maybe it was guardian angels," he says. I look up at the sky, wondering if my mom is somehow responsible. It's a nice thought and makes me smile.

"Well, if that's the case, mine sure do have a weird sense of humor."

He chuckles. "I like to believe that everyone comes into my life for a reason—either as a lesson or long-term. Only the passing of time reveals that. Like Finn. We've been friends since we were kids. The majority of the women I dated were nothing more than a lesson."

"And what did you learn?" I ask.

"If you have to chase someone for their attention, they aren't interested in you. Love has to go both ways for it to ultimately work out. It's why I don't waste people's time if I don't feel a connection."

"That's a nice perspective—learning a lesson. I've never thought about it that way." My ex comes to mind, but I keep that to myself. I've already spilled enough of my heart today, even if he's a great listener with zero judgment.

I glance at him at the same time he looks at me, and I smile but nervously turn my head. My body heats, and I know it's not from the blanket wrapped around me.

When the barn comes into view, I'm somewhat disappointed because I'm not ready for our time to end.

Levi pulls the reins until the horses come to a stop and then helps me off the sleigh. An older gentleman walks out of the barn and unhooks the horses while chatting with Levi.

Dasher runs around as Levi says his goodbyes, and then we walk to the truck that's parked on the side. Like a perfect gentleman, he reaches for the handle of the door but stops before opening it.

"Fallon," he mutters in a hoarse whisper. Carefully, he places his gloved palm on my cheek, then leans in and paints his lips across mine. I nearly melt as our tongues swipe together, and I groan against him. As much as I try to hold back, my body gives me away.

When we push apart, both gasping, I meet his gaze. "What was that for?"

He gently smiles and shrugs. "You looked like you needed it."

I lick my lips, wishing I could taste him again. "I did, or *you* did?"

Levi leans in and nibbles against my ear. "Well, considering you reciprocated…that's a question you need to ask yourself."

His scruff brushes against my neck and goose bumps trail along my skin.

Words escape me as Levi opens the door. Dasher climbs inside, and I follow. After we're buckled, we take off.

"Are you okay with us heading back to the shop? Just want to let my mom and sister know I'm leaving."

"Yeah, sure."

Before coming to Vermont, if anyone had told me considerate, sweet men like Levi still existed, I would've called them a liar. But here he is.

The right man at the wrong time.

Once the building comes into view, Levi slows and puts the truck into park.

"I'll be right back," he tells me with a wink and gets out.

I look at Dasher. "You might be the luckiest dog in the world."

He blinks at me, almost as if he agrees. Reaching over, I take my glove off and twirl his golden hair between my fingers. He repositions himself until he's halfway sitting on me.

"You're ridiculous. But I'm gonna miss you, buddy." I lift my arms, giving him the space he needs.

Five minutes later, Levi returns. "My mom and sister said you're welcome to help out any day of the week. Apparently, they're ready to ship me to Seattle and keep you instead."

I chuckle. "They're great. Your sister shared all sorts of juicy things about you."

He looks at me incredulously. "Of course she did. Well…" He hesitates. "Are you going to share with the class?"

I pretend to lock my lips and throw away the key. "Not a chance in hell."

"Don't make me march back in there and demand her to tell me," he warns.

"Go for it. Your threats don't bother nor intimidate me," I say with a shrug.

"I'll get it out of you."

"We'll see." I smirk, petting Dasher.

On the way to his house, I reach forward and turn on the radio. Holiday music lightly plays in the background, but this time, I don't immediately change it.

"Oh, this is my favorite song," he tells me, turning up the volume.

"Please Come Home for Christmas" plays, and I look out the window at the piles of snow on the side of the road as Levi sings along. He makes a show out of it, reaching and grabbing my hand. I laugh at his playfulness, enjoying the happiness radiating off him.

"I have a memory of my parents dancing to this song in the living room when we were putting up the tree," I tell him as the guitar solo starts.

"Mom was laughing so damn hard as Dad spun her around, dipping her, and then kissing her. I thought he'd drop her, but he never did."

"I can almost picture that."

I nod, listening to him belt out the final chorus.

"I swear, that's the shortest song of all time," I say when it ends.

"It really is." He puts his blinker on and then kicks his truck into four-wheel drive as we turn onto his road. The cabin sits at the top of the hill, and I take in how cozy it looks surrounded by the snow-covered evergreens.

Before we get out of the truck, Levi shifts and meets my eyes.

"I'm really sorry for pushing all this holiday shit on you, Fallon."

"Oh God, no. Don't be. I should be thanking you for putting up with my attitude and letting me stay here. Christmas still isn't my favorite holiday, but it's actually growing on me thanks to you."

"That's good enough for me. Ya know, since my entire personality depends on it." He shoots me a wink, nearly repeating the words I said to him when I first arrived.

I chuckle. "I'll never be able to change the fact that you're a real-life Santa. It's just who Levi White, the Christmas tree farmer, is."

"Not the first time I've been told that and I'm sure it won't be the last, either," he says.

We make our way inside and take off our coats. Levi feeds Dasher, and I kick off my boots.

"I'm gonna go take a shower," I tell him.

"Okay. I'll get dinner started. What are you in the mood for?"

My eyes trail up and down his body, and I drink him in. *Are you on the menu,* I want to ask, but instead, I say, "Surprise me."

"Will do."

I go upstairs, strip off my clothes, and get under the hot water. As I wash my hair, I relax under the stream and replay my day with Levi.

His kindness and hospitality is something I don't deserve but am so damn appreciative for it.

After I've finished, I get dressed and make my way downstairs.

Hearty aromas waft through the air, and my stomach growls. I enter the kitchen, and he looks at me over his shoulder. Dasher is lying on the floor at his feet.

"What did you decide?" I ask.

"I had some salmon in the freezer that my dad caught in Alaska. Serving it with black beans and roasted Brussels sprouts. One hundred percent gluten-free."

"The beans I'm on board with, but the Brussels sprouts I'll save for you." I give him a wary look.

"Have you tried them before?" he asks.

"No. I don't like the way they look or smell."

He bursts into laughter. "Sometimes, I have no idea what's gonna come out of your mouth."

"They look like little alien veggies when they're cooked."

"You're trying them tonight," he orders. "But I do have to warn you… your farts might stink."

Now, I'm laughing. "And you say I'm the unpredictable one! Also, ladies don't do that."

He glares at me. "*Sure,* right, right. If you hate them, I won't force you to eat them all."

"I'll try anything just once." The words linger in the air, and that's my rule in *and* out of the bedroom.

Levi flips the fish.

"Do you enjoy cooking?" I ask.

Levi laughs. "For you, I do. But when it comes to myself, I could eat a bowl of cereal and be satisfied."

My heart flutters at the thought of him doing this for me. "Me too. It's hard to make food for one person, especially for me. Don't really like leftovers either."

Levi's eyes nearly bug out of his head. "Seriously? Why not?"

"It's just never been my thing. I'll eat them only when I'm desperate."

"Not sure you'd survive living here. My mom makes so much food during the holidays, we're always sent home with airtight bags full of turkey, ham, and the works."

"Sorry, but you'll never change my mind about that."

"What if you didn't know it was a leftover, though?"

"Oh, I always know," I say matter-of-factly. "It tastes different."

He mischievously chuckles. "Whatever you say."

"Why are you laughing?"

"No reason," he singsongs.

I glare at him. "You've fed me leftovers, haven't you?"

"You didn't even notice! And I didn't know it was one of your... *quirks.*"

"It never came up because delivery doesn't exist here. But if you saw my fridge in Seattle, you'd judge me. It's where takeout goes to die."

"Oh, Fallon Joy. What am I gonna do with you?"

I smile wide. "Remember me forever."

"Don't have to worry about that, babe. You're unforgettable."

The oven timer goes off, and Levi grabs a mitt. Carefully, he slides the tray out, sets it on top of the stovetop, then removes the skillet from the heat. I enjoy watching him plate our meal.

"Wine?" he asks.

"Sure."

He grabs two glasses and opens the bottle. Once our glasses are filled, he slides into the stool next to me.

"What?" he asks as I look down at my plate.

"I seriously have to eat this?"

"Just one bite." He laughs. "Try it. You're almost worse than a kid."

I playfully smack him, then stab one with my fork. Before placing it in my mouth, I smell it. Then as Levi watches me, I open wide and pop it inside. The outside is crispy, and the inside is squishy, but it tastes...*not horrible.*

"Well? You didn't spit it out, so that must be a good sign?"

I pop my lips. "I always swallow the things I put in my mouth, whether good or bad. Not much of a spitter."

Levi nearly chokes, and I love catching him off guard. I pat his back. "You okay?"

He clears his throat and takes a big gulp of wine. "You're trying to kill me."

"These are actually really good. They're buttery. Not sure why I've always refused to give them a chance." I eat another.

"It's because you're stubborn," he quips.

"No denying that, but somehow, you've managed to make progress."

"It's my jolly nature." Levi shoots me a wink.

We continue making small talk while we eat. Randomly, I'll throw Dasher a piece of salmon, which he quickly gobbles up.

"Keep doing that, and you'll never be able to eat in peace again."

"Like it matters," I say with a laugh. "You've raised a beggar."

After we're finished, I offer to clean up, but Levi refuses to let me.

"Are you sure you're the real deal?"

"Huh?" He rinses off the plates and puts them in the dishwasher.

"A man who cooks and cleans. Who's nice to his mama. Single. Hardworking. Thoughtful. And has a golden retriever to match his energy. Do you realize you're an anomaly?" I can't even be mad or shocked at all the women who stopped him that day we went into town. They already knew he was a catch.

He chuckles. "Don't flatter me."

"I'm serious," I tell him. "What skeletons do you have hiding in your closet? Do you have a wife and kids in another country or something?"

Levi wipes his hand on a dish towel, then sets it on the counter. "Nope. Nothing in there but some cobwebs and handfuls of failed relationships. Probably some old ornaments and expired candy canes too. And that's the truth. I don't have anything to hide from you, Fallon. I'm an open book."

I search his face and can tell he's not lying. He has no reason to, but I still find it unbelievable someone hasn't won over his heart.

We go into the living room, and Levi turns on the TV but hands me the remote.

"My turn to shower," he says, and I nod.

I flick through the channels and land on a holiday movie because that's all that's on. It's not like I'm watching it anyway.

Once Levi is out of the shower, he comes downstairs to let me know he's going to bed.

"Good night, Fallon," he calls out.

"Night," I tell him. Dasher looks at me, then back at him before he follows Levi up the stairs. I stare at the ceiling, hating that I'm fighting a war within myself. And for what, exactly?

When the exhaustion takes over, I turn off the TV and make my way upstairs. As my feet touch the top floor, I stop and look at Levi's closed door. Placing my palm on the wood, I slowly turn the knob and walk in. The Christmas tree in the corner is lit, and Dasher's asleep on his dog bed. I take a few steps forward, my nerves getting the best of me.

I haven't walked into his room since that night we hooked up, but I've wanted to so damn bad.

Levi rolls over, and his eyes flutter open. He lifts the blankets without questioning why I'm in here. When I crawl in, he pulls me closer to his warm body. His strong arm wraps around my hip, but I spin around and face him.

When Levi's lips slowly part, I lean in and slide my mouth across his. The kiss deepens as our tongues tangle together, and I'm nearly breathless by the time I pull away.

"What was that for?" he asks.

"You looked like you needed it," I say, repeating the words he said to me earlier.

When I roll over, Levi's strong arm captures me, and his warm breath tickles my neck. Though I live with some regrets in my life, telling him our night together was a mistake is another one. If I could take it back, I would in a heartbeat, but maybe it's for the best.

CHAPTER SEVENTEEN

LEVI

DAY 12

WITH ONLY TWO days left before the festival this Saturday, the last thing I should be doing is taking a day off work. But it's exactly what I do.

Fallon's scheduled to fly out on Sunday, and I haven't been able to take her to the ski resort outside of town.

A part of me is taking her for selfish reasons because I want to spend more alone time with her, especially after yesterday's turn of events.

But I also want her to experience the slopes for her article.

After she crawled into my bed last night and kissed me, I knew the spark between us was still ignited. There's no denying our physical attraction and chemistry, but we have more than that sizzling between us.

The way she opened up to me, and shared personal details about her mom, drew me even closer. Not only has she embedded herself into my home but under my skin as well. It's hard to imagine what life will be like when she's gone.

"All packed?" I tap my knuckles on her door and smirk when I see Dasher lying on her bed while she shoves things into her bag.

"I think so."

"Great, we can head out then. Gotta take Dasher to my parents' first."

When Fallon walks past me, I grab her suitcase. "Let me."

"Okay, thanks." Her eyes meet mine as unspoken words float between us. Neither of us brought up the two kisses we shared yesterday, but waking up with her in my arms had me wanting to stay in bed with her until noon.

She lifts her computer bag and maneuvers it over her shoulder as Dasher and I follow her downstairs. Though she hasn't shared many details about her article, I hope she'll let her heart guide her. Once we drop off Dasher and chat with my parents for a few minutes, we hit the road. Fallon plays with the radio until she finds a station that isn't playing Christmas music, and I chuckle at how her avoidance has returned.

"You have to admit, some of it is just cringe."

"They're classics!" I argue.

She rolls her eyes. "Hard pass. I'd rather listen to Dasher's heavy breathing in my ear than 'Silent Night.'"

I gasp dramatically. "That's criminal. Take that back."

"Never!" She laughs, and it's the sweetest sound I've heard all day. As soon as I turn onto the road that leads to the resort, Fallon's eyes widen as the building comes into view. "That place is huge. And look at all that snow."

"It's a tourist favorite. The owners have invested a lot of time and money to keep it updated. The amenities are some of the nicest I've ever had. They get featured in several magazines every year for the best slopes in New England."

"I'll be the judge of that."

"You're so cynical."

"I have to be in this business. Otherwise, people would just buy me off or offer me free shit for writing a puff piece. Even though it's a lot of work to travel and deal with new environments, I take my job seriously. I want the readers to know that I'm always honest, and they can trust my word."

"You're probably one of a few journalists left like that," I say.

She shrugs. "Maybe. I just don't see the point of being a writer if I'm not going to be truthful. Why even bother?"

"Well, now I'm really looking forward to reading what you write about our town."

"Oh, once I leave, it won't be ready for a few weeks. My editor will go through it and add photos and captions. It takes me a few drafts, especially when I'm between jobs and traveling."

"Where are you going after here?" I ask as I pull into the guest entrance.

"I'm supposed to write about coffee roasters in Washington," I explain. "But that's not until January."

"That sounds more up your alley." I grin.

After I park, I walk around and open Fallon's door. Then I grab our bags and hand my keys over to the valet.

"Mr. White, how lovely to see you again!" Mrs. Shepherd smiles wide, walking around the counter to give me a hug.

"Likewise! It's been too long."

"I was wondering if you'd come visit me soon."

"You know my winter isn't complete until I see you." I shoot her a wink.

Mrs. Shepherd is a sixty-year-old woman who's worked here since I was a kid. While she's in upper management, the woman enjoys working the desk and greeting the guests.

"I set you up in the Snowball Suite."

"What's that?" Fallon asks next to me.

I almost warn Mrs. Shepherd about Fallon being a journalist but decide not to. I want her to enjoy herself without feeling as if she has to be professional anytime she leaves the room.

"It comes equipped with a full kitchen, fireplace, hot tub, and separate living room. There's also a balcony off the bedroom so you can watch the skiers."

"Sounds nice," Fallon says, and I know she's taking notes mentally.

"What time would you like your turndown service?"

"Let's do six," I tell her since it's already one, and we'll be leaving for dinner around that time. "Instead of two hot cocoas, can you send one coffee, please?"

"Of course." She continues typing on the computer. "Do you need an access code to the workout room or pool?"

"Yes, please. I'd like to show my guest around."

"No problem." Mrs. Shepherd grabs our keys and writes down our codes. "As you know, complimentary breakfast is from six to ten. Here's the number for equipment rentals or if you need a shuttle to the other ski lifts."

"Got it." I slide one key to Fallon and shove the other in my pocket. "Thank you so much."

"You're welcome. I hope you both have an amazing time." Mrs. Shepherd glances at Fallon with a wide smile. I've never shown up here with a woman, so I can only imagine what thoughts are going through her head.

I grab our bags and lead Fallon to the elevators.

"She was very nice," Fallon says as we wait.

"I've known her for most of my life. Sweetest lady you'll ever meet."

Once we get on and I press the button for the top floor, Fallon faces me. "This seems a lot like a romantic getaway."

"Well, it's a resort for couples and families. I wanted you to experience everything they had to offer, so I booked the best room."

"On such short notice? How'd you manage that?"

I smirk with a knowing shrug. "I have connections."

She snorts. "I'm sure you do. Is it one of those *stay thirty-eight times, get the thirty-ninth free* promotions?"

Barking out a humored laugh, I throw my head back at her reference. Of course I just pulled a random number out of my ass, but the fact that she's still thinking about it means something.

"Actually, number forty is the freebie. What are you doing next weekend?" I flash her a wink.

"Keep dreaming."

"You break my heart, Fallon Joy."

We arrive at our floor, and as soon as I open the door to our room, Fallon walks in and examines every inch of the place.

"What do you think?" I ask, setting our bags down on a bench.

"It's massive." She goes from room to room, then checks out the tub and kitchen. "Um...there's only *one* bed."

"It's a king-sized," I reassure her.

"Like that's ever stopped you from snuggling with me."

I chuckle, amused she's putting up this act, considering she's the one who initiates it every time.

"We should get ready to hit the slopes so we have time to see everything. The patio has a nice seating area with a firepit and bar."

"I've never skied, so bear with me."

"No problem. There are plenty of instructors."

"What? No, that's embarrassing."

"Hey, it's one of the perks. Newbies get free ski lessons with a professional. Or you can fall on your ass a hundred times and potentially break something, your choice."

She groans. "Fine."

While Fallon adds layers, I contact the equipment rental and ask about lessons. Once it's settled, I look her over.

"I rented all the gear for you," I tell her as she glances at my snowsuit, helmet, and goggles.

"I'm going to freeze, I just know it." She groans. I stand in front of her and grip her shoulders. "If you wear all that, by the time you suit up, you'll be sweating. Ski clothes aren't a joke, and I bet once you experience how warm it keeps you, you'll never wear anything else in the snow again. Trust me?"

She nods and her shoulders slightly relax.

"If you're not having fun, we'll end the lesson, but I just want you to experience it. Who knows, you might actually enjoy it."

"Let's not get ahead of ourselves."

I chuckle at her deadpan expression.

"Alright, let's go. We need to get your gear and meet the instructor at the bunny hill."

"Bunny hill?" she asks with a brow popped.

"It's cute. You'll see."

"My ass is numb," Fallon mutters as I help her up for the fifth time in twenty minutes.

"From falling or from the cold?" I tease.

"Both."

"You're doing great. Just take it really slow and focus on your balance."

The ski instructor worked with Fallon for an hour, but for the first thirty minutes, he yapped away about safety on the slopes and taught her how to snap her boots into the skis. The last thirty minutes were the hands-on lesson, and I was happy when it was over. I didn't like the way he kept touching her hips and making flirty comments. I was moments away from telling him to back off before the lesson was finally over, and it's a miracle I didn't.

Since then, I've been doing my best to teach her the basics. She's gone down the tiny hill a few times but gains too much speed, panics, and then falls.

"I'm going to stand behind you and slowly guide you down this time," I tell her, clicking out of my skis. "That way, I can catch you if needed."

"Now that sounds like fun," she quips.

"Don't fall on purpose," I warn. "You might take me out, and I'm not used to landing on my ass like you."

"Hey!" She swats at me, and I laugh when she stumbles into me.

I grip her hips and stand behind her, holding her tight as she slowly glides down the hill.

"This is embarrassing. Six-year-olds are skiing better than me." She looks out at the kids zipping down the beginner hill.

I lean down closer so she can hear me. "You're doing great, my love. Just focus."

She breathes out and slowly moves again.

Once she's halfway down the hill, I release my grip, and she glides faster, staying in complete control.

I follow, and when she nears the bottom, I notice she's trying to slow down before she topples through a bunch of little kids playing at the bottom.

"Fallon, turn!" I call out, chasing after her, knowing they aren't paying attention.

She squeals, shifting her body to miss them.

I meet up with her just as she turns and catches her as she falls. But she takes me down with her.

"Argh," I mutter as her knee gets awfully close to my groin. "You okay?" I ask when she doesn't move.

"Can I please be done now?"

I bellow out a laugh. "Yeah, you've given me enough bruises, I think."

Once she's up, she clicks out of her skis, and I carry both pairs to the rental place.

"So overall, not too bad, right?" I ask as we wait to turn everything in.

She shoots me a glare. "Two out of ten, but we'll see how sore I am later."

"Practice helps."

She points at herself. "Not a fan of the cold, remember?"

"How could I forget?" I grin. "Luckily, our room will be toasty when we get back."

Fallon offers me a smile as we slowly walk back to the resort.

I'd keep her warm all night with my face buried between her thighs, but I don't dare say that aloud.

Doesn't mean I'm not thinking it.

CHAPTER EIGHTEEN

FALLON

As soon as we're back in our room, I sigh in relief at how cozy and warm it is.

The fireplace is on, and two hot beverages wait for us on a tray. Thank God for turndown service.

Immediately, I grab the coffee and moan when I take a sip.

"Wow, this is good."

"It's Italian beans, apparently. They have a great café, and the food is delicious too. You hungry?"

"Starving."

"Good, I got us a reservation in forty-five minutes. Then I'll show you around the resort."

My mind's already exploding with mental notes I need to write down, but I need to clean up and change, so I'll have to wait to write my thoughts down until later.

I hear the shower running and am tempted to take a peek but decide against it. As much as I want to join him, I'm leaving in two days and don't need to add heartbreak to the list of things I take back to Seattle with me.

When Levi is done in the bathroom, I go inside and quickly step under the stream, washing off the sweat. Once I'm dressed and put on fresh makeup, I find Levi waiting in the living room.

"Wow." His eyes brighten. "You look beautiful."

"Thanks. You don't look too bad yourself."

"Well, that was *almost* a compliment," he mocks.

I roll my eyes, then stand in front of him and tug on his collar. His hair is finger-combed, and he smells like the beach. "You look very handsome. It's giving me *mountain man meets surfer* vibes."

"So damn mouthy." The corner of his lips curls up in amusement, but he's staring at my lips as if he wants to devour me.

"You'd be bored if I wasn't."

"I have no doubt about that."

Levi leads me to the elevator and down to the restaurant. It's decked out in Christmas decorations, and I count three trees on the way to our table. The lights are dimmed with flickering candles at each table as the fireplace roars. Garland and mini Santa Clauses line the massive mantel.

Even though I could do without the décor, the cozy romantic vibes are a nice surprise.

"You look nauseous," Levi says once we settle at our table.

"Just thinking about how this place makes your decorations look like child's play. I didn't think that was possible."

He looks around and smiles. "Honestly, I hardly notice it anymore. I'm used to everything looking like Santa's workshop during this time of year."

"I can see why the tourists would enjoy it, though. Especially kids. It's kinda magical."

"My parents took Lucy and me here every year when we were little. Even in the middle of our crazy season, they'd always make time to let us ski and enjoy the holidays without work."

"That's sweet."

"I guess add it to my long list of traditions. Going to Bennett's during the fall and Halloween season, cutting down a Christmas tree after Thanksgiving, and then a weekend away skiing. I think most locals do those things each year too. Well, between lots of shopping in the downtown square and going to the winter festival. In the spring and summer, there are also a lot of family-friendly activities."

"I wish my boss would've assigned me to visit in the summer. There's something nice about being outside and soaking in the sunshine."

He laughs. "We have tons of outdoor concerts. We'll take blankets for the lawn and drink mojitos all day while listening to awesome music. I like to go strawberry picking, but the farmers' markets are really popular, too. Oh and our Fourth of July parade and firework display are incredible. It's something I look forward to each year."

"Wow, it sounds like something is always going on," I say, not realizing how active they are year-round.

"Maybe you could ask to come back? Experience Vermont all over again. It's completely different, then."

His hopeful tone makes me frown.

"Yeah, maybe. Though I'm hoping this article will get me promoted to senior editor, which means less traveling."

"You don't like the jet-setter lifestyle?"

"I do, but I'd rather visit places for pleasure, ya know? When it's always for work, it kind of sucks the fun and spontaneity out of it."

"You, *spontaneous*?"

I playfully kick him under the table. "I'm only work-focused when I have to be."

A server interrupts our conversation to discuss the specials and hands over the wine menu. To my surprise, Levi orders a bottle.

"We're celebrating," he says.

"We are?" I ask, confused.

"You skiing and not breaking a bone. Or any of mine."

"Ha! Funny. But I'm not complaining."

"That's my girl."

"What do we plan on doing after dinner?" I wonder if he has any other surprises up his sleeve today.

"I thought we could just hang out by the fire or hop in the hot tub. Whatever you want. I'm up for suggestions."

"Both sound nice," I say sheepishly. The thought of being isolated in a romantic hotel room with him has my heart racing with anticipation. This man tests my willpower, and I wish I could throw my hesitations out the window.

"You should try the steak. It's some of the best in the state," he tells me as we look over the menus, and I notice the prices.

"This is expensive," I murmur.

"Don't worry. Guests staying at the resort get a fifty-percent discount."

"Oh." It makes me wonder about the cost of our room.

We order the same things—steak and veggies. Although I don't drink red wine often, he picked one I actually like.

"This place reminds me of the last restaurant my ex Blake took me to before he broke things off."

"Blake's a fucking moron."

I snort. "I was living in a false bubble and should've seen it coming. I just wanted us to be exclusive and for him to acknowledge that."

"Wait...you weren't?"

"*I* was. But he never wanted to make it official."

His jaw twitches. "And how long did you date?"

"Six months. He kept stringing me along, saying all the right things at the right times, buying me gifts, and showering me with countless compliments. I was certain he wanted to make things *official* because we hit it off so well. But I was very wrong and stupidly fell for his act."

"Christ. Was he a frat boy? What man doesn't make it known that you're his?"

My heart pounds at his words.

I lower my gaze. "A lawyer."

He breaks out in a humorless laugh. "Oh, Fallon."

"I know. Trust me. As soon as he hesitated and came up with some stupid excuse about not ruining a good thing, I should've walked away."

"It's not your fault," he reassures me, which only encourages me to keep talking.

"I really thought he was different, just busy with work. So I kept waiting, wanting to take our relationship to the next level. I honestly believed we were *together together* and just needed confirmation. I wanted to hear him say it, but when he didn't, I was gutted. He'd already met my family, and I'd met his. He took me to his cousin's wedding and introduced me to his nana! I didn't know putting a label on what we had would make him run. I thought I was in love, and it hurt to learn he was a player, and I definitely got played."

"Take it from a former fuck *man*, if we want a woman, we'll make it known and do whatever it takes to win her over. You know the saying *if he wanted to, he would*? Because that's exactly it. He didn't appreciate what he had. You deserve better than that, Fallon. Asking him that question, as hard as it might've been and as much as it hurt later, helped you in the long run. Sorry bastard."

I suck in a deep breath, taking his words to heart. Then I smile. "*Former*, huh? When did that change?"

"About twelve days ago when a brunette bombshell entered my life. Weirdly enough, I haven't been able to get her out of my head ever since she maced me."

My cheeks burn as I hold back a laugh. "I'm tempted to add that into my article."

"Do you need a replay of events? I can model naked for you."

This time I don't hold back and bellow out a hearty laugh. It feels good to be around someone who makes conversation easy and fun.

I tap my temple. "Trust me, I still have that visual right up here. Engrained forever."

"That seems like an invasion of privacy."

I shrug with amusement. Considering his tongue's been between my legs and ass cheeks, the man has no room to talk.

When our food arrives, I immediately dig in and realize just how hungry I am.

"I think this is the best steak I've ever had," I tell him.

"Told ya. It complements the wine nicely too."

"It almost helps me forget this place looks like a neatly arranged storage warehouse for Santa's toy factory."

"Have another glass, then," he taunts. "Or bottle."

"I just might. But considering my business card was canceled, it's not happening. They get weird about alcohol when I file for a company reimbursement."

"Fallon, I'd never take you on a date and make you pay. You know how to bruise a man's ego."

"This is a *date*?" I meet his eyes.

He looks flabbergasted that I even asked. "Nice restaurant, fancy dinner, you looking hot as fuck. Of course it's a date. You must *really* think I'm a serial one-night stand kind of guy."

"Aren't you?"

He leans forward with his elbows resting on the table and clears his throat. "The last woman I slept with was six months before I met you, and I broke it off when I found out she was married. The woman before that was four months earlier. She lied about having children. I love kids and would've had no problem being with a single mom, but she lied to my face, and I don't fuck with liars. The woman before her, I took out a few times before she told me she was moving to Japan for work. I can deal with long-distance, but she had no plans to ever come back, so it was pointless to try. We ended on good terms, and she's now married with a baby on the way."

I gulp at the realization of how wrong I've been about him.

"And the numerous women before her didn't work out for one reason or another, but I wasn't sleeping with them for sport. Have there been a few one-night stands? Yes. But I didn't plan them. Either they ghosted me or ended up dating someone else instead. Most couldn't handle my work schedule, and I'd rather find that out sooner than later. If I wasn't interested for any reason, I've always been straightforward about it. I've *never* led a woman on and have always been honest. That is..." He pauses, staring intently into my eyes. "*Until you.*"

My heart's beating so hard that I'm shocked he can't hear it. Licking my dry lips, I attempt to ask him what he means, but he continues.

"Because I haven't told you how I really feel about you. I've been holding back, respecting your wishes to pretend our night together didn't happen. But every damn day, I bite my tongue so I don't break down and beg you to stay—even if for a couple more weeks. I'm not ready to say goodbye to you, yet. I'm only telling you now because I don't want you leaving here thinking I used you or that you aren't worthy enough for me to fight for you. I'm not your ex because I'd never let you go if you were really mine."

Tears fill my eyes as I choke back a sob. I'm too stunned to speak as I soak in his every last word.

No man has *ever* allowed his heart to speak to me like this. My chest rises and falls as the world around us briefly disappears.

Levi brushes his thumb over my cheek, catching a tear. "Who knew the grinch could cry?"

I choke out a chuckle and shake my head, knowing how hard I've fallen in such a short time. This is his fault for being so incredible.

With my next breath, I find the courage to say my next words. "Ask me to stay."

I'd happily reschedule my flight if he wanted me here. Though I feel like I'd be a Debbie Downer during his holiday since my family stopped celebrating years ago, I'd rather spend it with him than be depressed and alone.

His face splits in two as he grabs my hand and rubs circles over it.

"Fallon Joy, will you stay and be my date for New Year's Eve?"

"Hmm...I'll have to check my schedule," I taunt, though it's wide open.

He leans forward, his voice in a low whisper so no one else can hear. "Not to bribe you, but I'd make it worth your while. First, I'd wine and dine you. Then we'd ring the new year in as I fucked you raw and hard to the sound of fireworks."

Jesus Christ.

"Okay, I'm convinced." I beam.

Levi sits back and waves his hand in the air.

"What are you doing?"

"Getting the check and our desserts to go. I'm not wasting another minute not being inside you."

As soon as Levi unlocks the door, his mouth and hands are on me. Though I don't know what this all means in the long-term, all that matters right now is having more time with him. With my office closing for the holidays, I can easily stay with him a couple more weeks.

"Fuck, Fallon. I want you, baby."

"I'm yours."

He lifts me, and my legs wrap around him as he pushes me against a wall. "Say it again."

I smile against his mouth. "I'm yours, Levi."

"Goddamn right you are." He cups my ass and grinds his erection against my core. "About to dedicate every one of your orgasms in honor of Brad."

I laugh. "Blake."

"Don't say his name. You scream mine and *only* mine."

"Is that jealousy I hear? It's giving me *possessive murder-y* vibes."

"You're just now realizing that? I thought you were a Crime TV junkie."

"Is this where you finally admit you're going to bury me in the yard once you kill me?"

"The only thing I'm burying is my dick inside your sweet cunt. Now let me hear you scream my name."

He brings me to my feet, then kneels, tugging my pants down to my ankles.

"Where are your underwear?" Licking his lips, he stares up at me.

"I forgot to pack them."

"Scandalous, but I know you're lying." He helps me step out of my shoes and pants, then tosses them aside. "Spread your legs. You need to be punished for being so damn naughty."

At his order, I do and wait with heavy breaths for what he's going to do to me.

His hands slide up my body, and he squeezes my thick thighs. "I fucking love your legs, baby."

My entire body buzzes as he makes his way between them and captures my clit with his teeth. Then he dives in like a starved man.

Over and over, he brings me to the edge, licking, sucking, fucking my pussy with his long fingers, but then stopping right before I come.

"Levi!" I scream in frustration after he brings me to the edge for the fourth time, denying my release.

He thumbs my clit, grinning up at me with my arousal covering his chin.

"Punishment, my love. I'll give you one when I think you deserve it."

"That's cruel," I hiss, ready to do it myself.

As if he can read my thoughts, he pins my wrists to the wall. "The truth shall set you free."

Groaning out in frustration, I surrender. "I left my panties behind on purpose."

He shoves two fingers deep inside, causing me to gasp while my back flies off the wall.

"Because you knew I'd notice."

"I thought it'd be one less thing for you to remove."

"Sounds like you were planning to seduce me." He stands, then tips my chin until our eyes meet.

I grin. "Did it work?"

He brushes my lips with his, soft and gentle at first, then swipes his tongue with mine. The scratch of his facial hair shoots shivers down my spine. I can't tell whether I like it more against my thighs or mouth, but either way, I'm addicted.

"All you have to do is ask, and I'll give you anything you want. No more games, Fallon."

His words have me in a puddle of emotions as I hear the tenderness in his voice.

After what I've put him through since I arrived, I'm shocked he isn't running in the other direction.

"I never claimed to be good at dating."

He smiles. "That's what I adore about you."

"My inexperience?"

"Your vulnerability. You carry a shield in front of you, but little by little, you've opened up and let me in. The closer I get to your heart, the further I fall."

Before I can respond, he cups my face and crashes his mouth over mine. I melt into his touch and moan.

"For the next two weeks, you're mine. Got it?"

"Yes," I whisper. "God, yes."

He lifts me again and carries me to our room. As soon as he sets me on the edge of the bed, I rip off my shirt and bra. He quickly undresses, then he joins me on the mattress.

I move to the middle and spread my legs. He's already hard and thick, stroking his shaft as he pushes against my entrance.

"You've ruined me for any other woman, Fallon Joy. There'll never be another like you."

He thrusts into me, and I moan in instant pleasure.

Our legs and arms tangle together as our bodies wreak havoc on each other. I've never been with a man who puts my pleasure first, who seeks out my orgasms and tells me exactly what I do to him.

He's the one who's going to ruin *me*.

"Don't stop, Levi," I plead while he's buried deep inside, torturing my clit and pinching my nipple. This man is the epitome of a skilled multitasker.

"On all fours, my love. I'm about to go so goddamn deep, you'll feel me in your throat."

Jesus.

Quicker than I'd like to admit, I flip over and stick out my ass. He gives it a hard smack before kneeling between my legs and pushing back in.

"Fuck, Fallon. You're so tight and perfect."

He snakes an arm between my legs and rubs my clit.

"Should we try to beat our record, baby?"

"Oh God. I'm still recovering from that," I say with a smile.

"Your cunt takes me so well, sweetheart."

"It's so deep, fuck."

"That's right, baby. Now give me that orgasm I earned."

And within seconds, I do.

"Shit, I'm close," he murmurs once I've come down from my high. "Get on your knees."

I blink, trying to catch my breath to obey. As soon as I get on the floor, I open my mouth and stick out my tongue.

"As much as I would love that, I'm not coming in that pretty mouth tonight. I still owe you that pearl necklace."

My face heats, and he shoots me a wink, stroking himself fast and hard.

Moments later, he growls out his release and covers my throat and chest in hot bursts.

"Fuck, aren't you a gorgeous sight?" He shoves his thumb between my lips, and I taste my arousal on it.

"Let's get in the shower and clean you up, sweetheart."

Our mouths crash together, then he lifts me.

"And then, we can christen that hot tub."

CHAPTER NINETEEN

LEVI

DAY 13

"I NEVER WANT to leave this bed," Fallon murmurs as I hold her naked body against mine.

"Me either, sweetheart. But I gotta get back to the farm. We have a lot to do before the festival tomorrow, and I need to catch up from taking off."

"What time's check-out?" she asks.

"Ten. Why?"

"That gives us an hour..." She flashes a smirk, then lowers under the blankets and settles between my legs. I'm not sure what our future holds, but I look forward to seeing where it goes.

Especially if this is how she begins our mornings.

"And here I thought you only needed coffee to start your day."

She giggles as she worships my cock, licking and sucking, working me up so much that I have to focus hard on not blowing my load in five seconds.

Twisting my fist in her wild mane, I guide her mouth up and down my length as she massages my balls. Her wet moans fill the room as I groan out her name.

"Fallon, baby..." My staggered breathing comes out in harsh pants. "That feels so goddamn good."

Once I'm teetering on the edge, she climbs between my legs and settles my erection between her thighs.

"Such a good girl," I tell her, pressing a finger between us and rubbing her needy clit. "Take what you need, my love."

I play with her tits as they bounce in my face, then lean up and pull a nipple between my lips. I roll my tongue around it and pinch it between my teeth, causing her to yelp as she continues to ride me.

Being with Fallon is better than I imagined, and while we haven't discussed what will happen beyond New Year's, I'll take what I can get.

The truth is, I want more, *much* more.

But I'll wait for her to initiate that discussion.

"You better be careful, Fallon Joy. I'm already getting addicted to your pussy."

Moments later, we're coming undone together, and that's when I know for sure that I don't ever want to let her go.

As I get ready for work, Fallon soaks in the tub, tempting me to skip another day, but I can't. With more tourists in town for the festival, the farm will be swamped.

"I'm sorry I have to leave." I lean into the tub and brush my lips against hers.

"It's okay. I have plenty of emails to catch up on and writing to do. Plus, my body's a *little* sore."

Smirking, I lower my hand and cup her breast. "I bet it is."

She swats my arm. "Go. Are you leaving Dasher here?"

"Yeah, is that okay? I won't be able to keep an eye on him, and I don't want to lock him up."

"It's fine."

"I'll text you when I can." I kiss her forehead, feeling guilty and sad about having to go.

"Have a good day," she calls out.

I find Dasher lying on my bed and give him a quick pep talk. "Be good for Fallon. I'll see you later, buddy."

He licks my hand, and I laugh.

As soon as I get to the farm, I notice the full parking lot and see a line of people standing outside the shop.

It's going to be crazy as fuck.

When I walk in, Mom greets me with a wave. She's all smiles as she helps customers check out. Lucy's behind the counter, handing out baked goods.

"Hey, sis."

"Get back here and make yourself useful."

I bark out a laugh. "You gonna come help me cut down trees, then?"

She gives me a murderous look that tells me to get lost.

I grab gloves and an extra walkie-talkie from the office, then make my way outside. I do a quick walk around and see if any areas are struggling to keep up with the demand. We have a record number of employees here, so I'll help wherever needed.

I help a dozen customers load their trees and tie them to their roofs or truck beds. Christmas music blasts through the outdoor speakers, and it's impossible not to think about Fallon and her distaste for it.

At first, I thought it was weird that anyone could hate the holidays as much as she does. But now I understand her reason, and it's completely valid. With the anniversary of her mom's passing coming up, I'm going to do whatever it takes to be there for her the best I can. Though I can't say I know how she feels, I can listen if she wants to talk or help distract her if she prefers.

Either way, I've blocked the day off just for her.

I plan to make New Year's special for her and give her a new memory to hold on to.

I finally get the chance to check my phone and smile when I see texts from Fallon.

FALLON

I think you have some new competition.

Then she sends a pic of Dasher snuggled up to her in bed, one of his paws on her chest. The little fucker is smiling too.

LEVI

Tell him he better get off my woman before I remove every one of his paws.

FALLON

Levi White!

I chuckle.

LEVI

Are you having a good day?

FALLON

Worked after you left and came to your bed because I missed you.

LEVI

I miss you too. We should go out for a drink once I'm done. You can experience the nightlife, and I can kick your ass at darts.

Though I'll be exhausted and the festival is tomorrow, I'm not passing up the chance to have some fun and show her off. I can function with as little as three hours of sleep, so it'll be worth it.

FALLON

You sound pretty confident...but okay, I'll take you up on that offer. Loser has to give the other a mind-blowing orgasm.

I arch my brow, amused by her flirting.

LEVI

If you want my mouth between your legs, all you have to do is ask.

FALLON

Oh, I'm going to enjoy EARNING it when I win.

LEVI

Getting the chance to eat your pussy? Babe, that's a win for both of us.

FALLON

😵

She sends an eye-roll emoji, and I picture her doing that very thing.

Then she sends a shot of her chest, the tops of her breasts peeking out of her tank top. I can't see her full face, just her sweet lips as she sticks her tongue out at me.

LEVI

Your ass is in major trouble now.

My cock strains against my jeans, and I groan. The last thing I need while chopping down trees is an erection. Then having to tell customers, "*Merry Christmas*," as I imagine shooting my load all over Fallon's tits.

FALLON

You gonna punish me?

Fuck, she's testing my patience.

Where the hell did this Fallon come from, and how do I keep her?

LEVI

All night long.

FALLON

Looking forward to it, Mr. White.

I shake my head and force my phone into my pocket so I don't sext her all damn day.

After another few hours, I finally get a break to eat and use the bathroom. Just as I walk into the shop, I see Finn and Oakley walking around with their arms full.

"Hey!" I pull Finn in for a hug. "What are you guys doing here?"

"My fiancée is buying the entire place out," he muses, and I chuckle at her basket full of cookies and gifts.

"No looking! I got something in there for Fallon, and I don't trust you not to spoil it," Oakley says, covering it up.

I grin. "You did? That's nice of you."

"Of course. I'm hoping I can sweet-talk her into staying. It'd be nice to have another woman to hang with who isn't a Vermonter. We can bond over being from the West Coast and all the weird shit you guys do and say."

"I managed to convince her to stay through New Year's, but I don't think she'll be able to stay longer than that," I reply sadly.

"Really? That's great," Finn says.

"That gives me more time to tell her all the reasons she should stay," Oakley adds.

I wish it were that easy.

"I'm taking her to the pub tonight if you wanna join us? Probably get there around eight."

They look at each other and smile. "Yeah, we'll meet ya," Finn says.

"We can chat about the wedding, too!" Oakley's eyes light up.

Grinning, I slap his shoulder. "Awesome, see ya there. I gotta get back to work."

"Damn!" Finn whistles as Fallon makes another bull's-eye. "She's kicking your ass."

Fallon smirks wickedly.

"I think she's cheating," I deadpan.

"How do you cheat at darts?" Oakley defends.

"I don't know...but I'm gonna figure it out." I watch as she takes another shot and again, hits the center.

Oakley cheers loudly for Fallon, and they high-five. Somehow this round became a game of boys versus girls, and they're killing it. My friends have welcomed her into their lives so easily, it's impossible not to think about the long term.

"Good luck..." Fallon says as she hands me the darts. "You're gonna need it."

I give her a side-eye, no longer playing just for orgasms, but because I'm competitive too.

As soon as I take my stance, Fallon stands next to me, sipping her drink. When I look at her, she flashes a mischievous grin.

"Yes?" I ask.

She shrugs, the alcohol effectively loosening her up, but not enough to affect her aim.

"Go sit, I don't trust you so close to me."

Fallon giggles. "I'm not doing anything."

"You're trying to distract me."

"*Noooo*," she stammers. "If that were the case, I'd take off my shirt and do a few jumping jacks."

My mind immediately brings that visual to life.

"Go to the table," I warn playfully. "Or I'll have to call a foul."

"Go ahead. I'll call traveling, then."

Finn snorts behind us.

"That's basket—" I shake my head at her wrong sports reference. "Never mind. Stand behind me, or you forfeit."

She scowls and finally moves out of my vision.

"Stay focused, man," Finn encourages. "If we win, I get a BJ."

"*Finn!*" Oakley scolds, smacking his arm, and my concentration flies out the window.

But then I remember, if I lose—I get to give Fallon a *mind-blowing* orgasm, and that sounds better than Finn's BJ.

"Fuck it." I slam the darts on the table and grab Fallon's hand. "Be right back," I tell Finn and Oakley while dragging her behind me.

"What are you doing?" she squeals, trying to keep up as I hustle down the hallway toward the bathrooms.

"Marking off one of your *Never Have I Evers*."

Sex in a public place.

"*Here*?" she whisper-hisses.

I pull her into the unisex bathroom and lock the door. Luckily, it's only a one-stall, but the bar is packed, so it won't be long before someone's knocking.

"Jeans to your ankles, baby. We gotta do this quickly."

"Is this *you* forfeiting?" she teases as she unbuttons and lowers the zipper.

"Call it whatever you want as long as I get to taste you." I push her against the door and move her feet as wide as they'll go. "I have a question to ask you first."

"What's that?"

"Come with me as my date to the festival tomorrow?" I ask, probing her entrance with my finger and coating it with her juices.

"What? I thought I was already going with you?"

"As Fallon, the *journalist*."

"What's the difference?" she asks.

I drop to my knees, lick up her slit and twirl my tongue over her clit. "I want everyone to know that while you're here, *you're mine*."

"That's ridiculous. I still have to work. The festival is the main reason I'm here," she explains between panting and pulling my hair.

I continue eating her delicious cunt and bringing her closer to the edge, but not quite over it.

"Say you'll be my date, Fallon." I shove two fingers inside her tight core. "Say yes, and I'll let you come."

"That's blackmail," she hisses, arching her hips to meet my mouth.

I reach up and palm her breast before plucking a nipple. Then I lean back and continue my sweet torture with my fingers.

"Call it whatever you want, sweetheart. But if you want this orgasm, you'll say the words I want to hear."

I want to hold her hand and kiss her without people thinking she's being unprofessional. They won't think twice about it if they know we're together. Plus, I don't want any asshats hitting on her.

She grinds down on my palm, desperately trying to do it herself. I press tender kisses above her clit, and she groans out in frustration as she attempts to shove my head lower.

"You're so needy, my love." I tease her clit for a few seconds, building her pleasure before backing away. "I want everyone to know you're taken," I explain.

Regardless of our time limit, she's mine to keep as long as she's in my house.

"Levi, please...I was so close."

"I'll give you exactly what you need, baby. Just say—"

"Fine! *Yes.* Yes, whatever you want. Now touch me," she demands, rocking her hips and seeking my mouth.

Such a good girl.

I spread her folds and dive in, sucking and licking, building her up over and over until her breathing halts and she screams out my name. Her juices cover my mouth and chin, but I don't care. I take everything she gives me.

"So fucking perfect, Fallon."

Standing, I cup her face and slip my tongue between her lips so she can taste her sweetness. I quickly help her clean up and pull on her jeans.

"Do you think they're going to know what we were doing in here?" she asks.

I smirk without apology. "The whole bar heard you."

"Levi, you're joking." She looks horrified.

"I welcome it. At least they'll know you're mine." I shrug, unlocking the door.

"Oh my God." She palms her face. "They're going to think I'm an unethical journalist."

"Nah, but they might think you're paying me top dollar for sex."

She playfully smacks my arm, but I catch her wrist and pull her body to mine. Brushing loose strands of her dark hair off her face, I hold her. "I guess you should've been more careful whose house you broke into and, more importantly, whose bed you picked. Because now I've claimed you, Fallon Joy."

CHAPTER TWENTY

FALLON

DAY 14

I WAKE up with Levi's cock pressing into my back, and there's no way that I can deny myself of him. We're greedy, animalistic, and fuck like the world will end tomorrow. If it did, I'd die a happy woman.

We lie in each other's arms, completely satiated, but we can't hide in bed all day. After Levi gets up and jumps in the shower, Dasher flies onto the bed and attacks me with licks.

"Oh my God," I say, trying to push him away, but he's too heavy. His tail wags, slapping against me, and I can't stop laughing as he nearly topples me. He plops down, and his cold nose brushes against my arm.

When he looks up at me with his brown eyes, I gently pet him. "Are you glad you get to annoy me for two more weeks?" I ask, with a laugh. I'm not naïve and know this time will fly by too.

My heart lurches forward when I think about it. Levi's company during this time of year has been my saving grace, and I can't imagine spending these two weeks holed up in my tiny apartment alone. That actually sounds awful. However, it's what past Fallon wanted. So much has changed.

I swallow hard, thinking about everything between Levi and me.

That's when I realize I'm fiddling with my mom's necklace. I look down at it, noticing the clasp is facing forward, and smile. Making a wish, I give it a kiss and move it to the back. It's a silly thing my sister and I used to do when we were kids. She used to tell me that every time it was backward, Mom was sending an *I love you and a hello* from heaven. The thought of it always comforted me.

After I crawl out of bed to get dressed, Dasher resettles himself in the middle of the mattress. I put on my heaviest sweater, jeans, and boots since we'll be outside enjoying the festival. The day I've been counting down to for weeks.

When Levi walks into the bedroom with a towel wrapped around his waist, I bite the corner of my lip. He takes a few steps forward, and I trail my finger down his chest and tug on the material.

"Don't start something you won't be able to finish, babe," he says, and I pout, knowing we have to get going.

"I'm taking a rain check on that cock," I whisper as he slides his lips across mine.

"I look forward to it."

As he gets dressed, I take Dasher outside and let him run out some of his energy. Then I give myself a pep talk, trying to turn on the journalist inside me because I'll have to be on my A game today. Especially now that everyone in town knows my name and why I'm here, but I also told Levi I'd be his date.

After Dasher is finished, we go inside, and Levi is making coffee.

"I thought we could eat there," he suggests. "There are lots of options and Lucy told me there is a gluten-free food truck there this year."

"Really? That's actually cool. I usually go for the mystery meat on the stick. It's the safest option."

Levi fills a small travel mug, then hands it to me. "Ready to get going?"

"Yep," I say, grabbing my phone so I can take notes while we walk around. While Levi puts a Santa hat and holiday-themed dog coat on Dasher, I hurry and apply some ruby-red lipstick..

On the way there, I sit right next to Levi in the truck. Dasher is in the back seat, taking advantage of having the whole thing to himself.

As we turn onto the country road that leads to town, Levi glances over at me. I love the heat in his gaze when our eyes meet and how my body instantly responds.

I shoot him a mischievous grin and guide my hand up his thigh. His brow pops up as I brush my palm over his cock that's steadily growing hard.

"What are you doing?" he asks when I free his thickness. Repositioning myself, I place my hot mouth on the tip and roll my tongue around.

"I'm cashing in my cock rain check. Keep your eyes on the road."

"Fuck, such a good girl," he groans out as I slide farther down on him, nearly choking.

"I like praise, but you know I'm your naughty girl," I admit, licking down the bottom of his shaft.

"Hell yeah, my only regret is not being able to have that pussy right now." Levi huffs, slightly repositioning the seat to give me more space. The speed of the truck slows to a near crawl. At this rate, we might make it to the festival tomorrow.

Using my hand, I stroke and suck, loving how he throbs in my mouth. Levi wraps my long hair around his fist, guiding my head up and down. I'm so goddamn turned on, my panties are going to be soaked, but I don't care. His grunts encourage me to keep going.

"Fuck, Fallon." His breathing is ragged, and my eyes nearly tear up, but I continue slamming him as far back in my throat as I can.

"Eyes on the road," I remind him, knowing he's close but is also holding back. "I'm going to suck the Christmas spirit out of you. Maybe it'll get me through this festival."

He moans but also chuckles.

"*I'm. Close*," he says between gritted teeth, holding the steering wheel with a white-knuckle grip. I slow my pace to a painful crawl. "Fallon," he whispers. His thighs tense, then he releases into my mouth. I drink him down, enjoying how he tastes, and lick up every last drop.

"Delicious. Thanks for breakfast."

"Anytime. You're going to get heavily rewarded for that later."

"Oh, I can't wait." I laugh as Levi waits for his erection to subside. Ten minutes later, he puts my favorite part of him away.

"That's a first for me," he admits.

"Really?" I ask. "Me too. I like that we can share things like that."

"Fuck, me too," he admits. "Might as well make a sex bucket list and start marking them off."

I chuckle. "How many do you think we can complete before January second?"

"I dunno, but I'm up for the challenge."

And I really like the sound of that.

As we drive, I finish my coffee, happy for the caffeine. When the town finally comes into view, I'm shocked by how much traffic there is. The parking lots are full, and after we circle the block a few times, I'm concerned we won't find a spot.

"I can drop you and Dasher off at the entrance, then meet you?"

I nod, popping my hat on my head before he slows and lets us out. Dasher looks adorable in his Christmas gear, and of course, the leash looks like it's a line of lit tree lights.

As he sniffs around the sidewalk and snow, random people stop and tell me how cute he is. He's such an attention seeker and gets pets from every person who compliments him.

I stand at the giant archway, trying to take in the ambience of the crowd and the smells of the food that float through the air. Moments later, strong arms wrap around my waist from behind, and I turn, wanting to greet him with a kiss.

As if he reads my hesitation, he leans in and whispers in my ear. "I don't give a fuck who sees us together, babe. I know what I said yesterday, wanting you to be my date, but I'm letting you call the shots in public."

I swallow, nodding with a smile and softly press my lips against his. He moans against my mouth, running his fingers through my hair.

"You're mine, too, Levi," I say, wanting him to understand that I want all these women to know he's with me. At least for now.

When we pull apart, I smirk, then grab his hand.

"I'll take him," Levi offers, so I give him the leash.

A few kids dressed as Santa's elves greet us as we enter, and a photographer captures everyone's pictures. Levi puts his arm around me and pulls me close as Dasher sits in front of us. Once the photo is taken, I'm handed a ticket and told that we can pick it up at the Chamber of Commerce booth.

As we walk through the crowd, every local greets us both by name.

Some notice our hands interlocked, and others don't, but no one makes a big deal out of it. The pathways are wide, but a lot of people are already here, and it's early.

"What time is the tree lighting?" I ask Levi when we find the food truck with the gluten-free goodies. I'm tempted to order one of each.

"Six on the dot. My mom is supposed to give a speech, and she said she expected me to support her from the front row," he explains.

"So we'll need to find seats early?" I ask, and he nods.

When we finally make it to the window, I order several pastries. Levi gets a few too.

"Not bad," he tells me, biting into a miniature pumpkin pie. "If I didn't know it wasn't made with flour, I'm not sure I'd notice."

"Right!" I agree around a mouthful, gobbling it up like I haven't eaten in days.

As we walk past some of the craft tables, I spot Oakley with her paints and canvas. Levi sees her at the same time, so we make our way over to her.

"Oh my God!" She squeals, then hugs me. "You're the first distraction I've welcomed all day. How are you two?" She looks back and forth between us, and I'm almost embarrassed about what happened last night. They both knew we fooled around in the bathroom, and after we returned, we basically called it a night. Finn was ready to get home anyway, though.

Levi and I meet each other's eyes. "Great," we say in unison.

"Ahh, saying the same things at the same time. That's a good sign," she teases.

Levi sees Finn across the way and excuses us.

"I forgot to chat about you staying longer yesterday. That's exciting."

"Yeah, I'm looking forward to spending New Year's here. I just rescheduled my flights, and it's official."

She gives me a small smile and hesitates. "Now, I don't want to get in your business or anything, and I don't need any details whatsoever, but when you get home, and if things don't feel right...listen to your heart."

I search her face, trying to read her expression.

"I almost didn't and it would've turned out to be the worst mistake of my life," she admits, and I see the engagement ring sparkle by the reflection of the sun.

"I will," I say. "I promise."

"Oh, I almost forgot," Oakley says, pulling a small package from her oversized purse. She hands it to me.

"What's this?" I ask.

"Just a small Christmas gift."

"Thanks, but I didn't—"

"Just open it already," she says. "It's nothing big."

I rip off the bright-colored paper and open a box that's the size of my palm. Inside is a snow globe. I hold it up to get a better look, then gasp. "It's the Christmas tree farm."

Oakley grins. "So you can take the farm back with you to Seattle."

As hard as it is, I push my emotions back and give her a hug. "Thank you."

She squeezes me tight, and I slide it into my oversized coat pocket.

Before I can say anything else, Oakley pulls me around to show me what she's painted so far. My eyes widen in shock as I look at a night scene of the gigantic tree that she has a perfect view of.

"I've pretty much got most of it done. I just need to fill in the lights on the tree, the crowd, and other small details, and then it's finished," she explains.

"You amaze me." I laugh, almost envisioning what the scene tonight will look like. "The best I can do is an uneven stick figure."

Moments later, Finn walks up with a holiday cup and hands it to Oakley.

"What were you two talking about?" he asks, placing a sweet kiss on Oakley's lips.

"Painting." Oakley shoots me a wink, and I appreciate her kindness.

"Well," Levi says. "Lucy has a booth around here somewhere. I need to go say hello."

"She's on the far side, right in the middle of all the commotion," Oakley says.

"Good seeing you again, Fallon," Finn offers. "Keep him out of trouble."

"One can only try," I say.

"If you get bored, I'll be here all night," Oakley tells us, and we wave goodbye.

Levi falls in line beside me with Dasher in tow. "What did she say?"

I chuckle, but her words aren't ones I'll be forgetting anytime soon. "Nothing. Nothing at all. But she did get me a gift."

"Yeah?" he asks.

I pull it from my pocket and show him.

"It's perfect." He laughs, and I quickly steal a kiss.

Eventually we find Lucy who's selling hand-carved ornaments from the shop and boxes of White's famous gingersnaps by the dozens. She's busy as hell, so we wait in line for our turn to chat with her.

"It's those cookies," I say, seeing just how many people are buying. "Is it really a secret recipe?"

"Yep." He smirks.

"And you're not going to tell me?"

He leans in and whispers in my ear. "Not until there's a ring on that finger."

My heart flutters at the idea of marrying this man. But I know it's just a fantasy, and I'm getting way ahead of myself.

"You're a tease. But I did notice your wise choice of words. You said *until* instead of *unless*."

"Always so observant," he mutters, then winks.

I swallow just as it's our turn to order. Lucy squeals when she sees us holding hands. "Oh my God, it's my favorite non-couple."

Levi leans across the table and gives her a hug. She forces me to do the same, but I don't mind it. "Are you guys having fun?"

I nod as Levi places some cash in her tip jar. "Just wanted to say hey and tell you that you're a badass."

"Thanks, Levi. You're my favorite hype squad. But I'm closing this baby down once I sell out of everything."

"Then I guess we better leave you to it," he tells her.

After walking around for a few more hours, we find an empty park bench and sit. I pull out my phone and type away, writing down all my thoughts.

"You're so fast," Levi says, sitting back.

"There's so much to write," I say, going back to my phone. He doesn't rush me or ask any questions, and after an hour of nonstop typing in my phone, my wrists and fingers ache. I lock it and look over at him, and he's completely relaxed, happy even.

"You're done?"

"For now, I think. I'm hungry."

Levi checks the time and chuckles. "Oh yeah, it's time for lunch. I'll drop Dasher off with Lucy if you'd like to go to the deli. She brought cans of dog food for me, so I'll feed him too."

"That lemonade actually sounds really good."

"And being inside will give you a chance to warm up," he offers.

See, that's the thing about Levi—he's always putting me first.

After we feed and drop Dasher off with Lucy, we head toward the diner.

When we enter, Greta smiles wide and leads us to the same booth we sat in the first time. It feels like deja vu because we order the same things, but I'm grateful the conversation is different.

"So are you leaving?" Greta asks, refilling my lemonade. It's freshly squeezed, and if I could take a gallon home with me, I would. Levi glances up at me, and I give her a smile.

"After the new year," I proudly say, hoping she spreads the word.

"Ahh, well that's great news," Greta says, winking at Levi.

When she walks away, he smirks.

"You know she's going to tell everyone."

I grin. "That was the point."

"Mm. I like possessive Fallon. She's strategic." He leans forward. "And sexy as fuck," he whispers.

Levi and I finish eating, and soak up the heat until the restaurant gets busy. Once a line forms outside, he pays, then we return to the festival.

Levi gets a text and laughs.

"What?"

"Lucy asked if she could keep Dasher all day because he's helping her sell more items in his costume."

"That's hilarious," I tell him. "But he did draw a lot of attention when I was waiting for you earlier."

Levi quickly texts Lucy back and tells her that's fine.

"Do you want to ice skate?" he asks as we pass a small rink that looks like it was brought here just for the event.

"That would be a big no. I'm not great on regular skates or ice, so that actually sounds like a nightmare. I need my arms, hands, and wrists."

He chuckles. "Fair enough."

We continue walking around the festival, and I'm amazed by how they packed so much into such a small space. Before long, Levi lets me know that we should probably get situated for the Christmas tree lighting. We find seats right up front, but a crowd's already forming.

I stare up at the gigantic Christmas tree with amazement.

"It's sixty feet tall," Levi leans in and tells me. "Twenty feet shorter than the Rockefeller Center tree in New York."

"Wow," I say, taking my time to study it.

"Yep. It's probably seventy-five years old, and there are around fifty-thousand lights on it."

"I have so many questions."

He looks excited to hear that. "A whole crew volunteers to string it every year. Takes a month to get it ready for this event."

I pull my phone out and write down as many details as I can while Levi continues giving me more history. Several people stop by and chat with Levi and offer friendly hellos.

When I hear tons of chatter, I turn around, and there are people as far as I can see. I take a quick picture, shocked by how crowded it got.

Soon, the mayor steps on the tiny stage in his Santa suit and welcomes everyone.

"Wow, big crowd," he says, and laughter follows.

"I'd like to thank you all from the bottom of my heart for supporting this festival. I have a long list of people to thank, but I know that if I start listing them, then I'll forget someone and regret it. This event takes place every year because of the locals who donate their time and money and love this town more than anything. The spirit of Christmas will always thrive here as long as it continues in the same capacity as it has since the turn of the century. But, with that being said, this lighting wouldn't be possible without the help of the Whites, whose Christmas tree farm donates the tree every year, no matter what. So I'd like to ask Mrs. White to say a few words before the moment we've all been waiting for."

Levi's mom steps up, and she looks adorable in her heavy coat. She's wearing reindeer antlers and meets my eyes as she moves to the microphone.

"Hi, everyone. Thank you so much for the kind introduction. I just wanted to say a few words before we light this beast," she tells us, laughter erupting.

"It takes an army to do this every year, and the reality is thousands of other farms could donate something this size or bigger. But every year, we ask and offer to be the ones who provide this tree. Why? Some of you might ask. It's because sometimes the world is dark. Bad things happen to good people. The holidays may not hold happy memories, but horrible ones. Everyone is different and has their own reason for not liking the holidays. But when this tree lights up every year, it swallows all of that up. And even if the darkness disappears in their lives for only a moment, then I think it's worth it. My goal is to bring a glimmer of light and plant a seed of hope into the hearts of every person who sees it shine. I know it brings happiness to many people, and that's why we donate a tree every year. And we will do it as long as this town will allow us to. Thank you, it's an honor."

The crowd erupts into applause, and they stand as I wipe tears from my cheeks. Levi's mom steps away, and he notices me caught up in my emotions and places his arm around me. It's the comfort I need.

She's right, and as the festival goes completely dark, the countdown begins. The anticipation is almost too much, and as the crowd bursts out into "We Wish You a Merry Christmas," the tree beams to life, casting warm light over the crowd.

Levi laughs, and I hoot and holler, admiring it in all its glory. I stare up at it, and the beauty of the lights twinkling in the darkness leaves me speechless.

"You okay?" he asks, and I nod, kissing his cheek.

"Just a little emotional."

As everyone stands around and takes pictures with the tree, we meet up with Levi's mom and dad.

"Your speech was beautiful," I offer. "Thank you."

"You're welcome, sweetie. Now"—she yawns—"I'm ready for bed."

"You two be careful driving home," Levi tells them with a kiss and a hug.

When we're alone, he turns to me. "There's one more thing I want to do."

"Okay, I'm game."

I follow him to the carnival rides, and we wait in line for the Ferris wheel. When we load up into the cart, Levi opens his arms for me to snuggle into.

"Are you getting cold?" he whispers.

"A little," I say as the cart begins to move. We go around a few times then we stop at the very top. Seeing the festival and all of the lights from above is absolutely breathtaking. I can't stop staring at the tree from a bird's-eye view. The yellow star on top shines bright and twinkles in the night.

I glance over at Levi, and he's watching me.

"What?" I ask.

He chuckles, moving closer. "You had the same look on your face as I did when I was a kid and would come to this festival. Utter awe."

I try to hold back a smile because he's right. "I think I understand the importance of it all now," I admit. A burst of goose bumps trails over my body as the realization hits me, and I've never been more ready to write than I am now.

"I'm proud of you," Levi tells me, painting his lips across mine

On the way out, we stop by Lucy's booth and grab Dasher.

"Might have to borrow him more often," she tells Levi.

"Or you can get your own dog."

"It's easier to take yours," she says with a laugh, and we say our goodbyes.

As our feet hit the sidewalk, I grab Levi's hand and interlock my fingers with his. Before we leave, he stops at the Chamber of Commerce booth. He slides a twenty across the table, and they hand him an envelope. He offers it to me and I open it, pulling out the photo of me, him, and Dasher from earlier today.

"Just so you'll never forget today."

I smile, wrapping my arms around his neck, and pull him in for a passionate kiss. "That's not happening, Levi. It's been a night to remember."

CHAPTER TWENTY-ONE

FALLON

DAY 22

MY EYES FLUTTER open as Levi spoons me. His breathing is low, and I know he's still sleeping. I'm not quite ready to get out of bed, so I lie there, enjoying his warmth and comfort. We actually slept in, and I'm thankful for the extra rest after spending Christmas Eve and Christmas with Levi's family.

The food was amazing, and just like he'd told me, his mom sent us home with ridiculous amounts of leftovers. I think her cooking might be the only thing that I'll eat the day after. It was the first time I actually celebrated Christmas since my mom's accident.

Today is the anniversary of her death.

December 27th.

The day my life changed forever.

The world wasn't as bright once she was gone, and I felt like I was grieving alone. At school, my friends treated me as if I were fragile, but then weeks later, it was like it didn't happen. Everyone else's lives seemed to go back to normal, and I was the only one who was still hurting.

Even now, I feel like that sometimes.

I've had people tell me that it's great to have had a mother worth missing, but how is that helpful? It's not. Some have even told me everything happens for a reason. As a thirty-year-old woman, I still don't see how my mother dying was *meant* to happen. It's a shitty thing to tell a kid. It's a shitty thing to tell anyone.

I grieve many things, but now that I've gotten older, I can't help but think about my nieces. They'll never really know how amazing their grandmother was. They won't ever feel her warm hugs or hear her infectious laugh. The kindness my mother gave to every person she ever met was unmatched. If I ever get married, she won't be there to witness it. If I have kids, she won't get to hold them. Not having my mom around to celebrate my life experiences feels like a continuous knife to the heart.

Typically, on this day, I drown myself in work. Focusing on keeping my mind and body as busy was always my priority, so I'd be exhausted when I got home and would crash. Not giving myself time to think about it has worked for me over the years. Is compartmentalizing my emotions the healthiest thing to do? Absolutely not.

Once my bladder screams out in protest, I wiggle out of Levi's hold and go to the bathroom. When I'm done, I look in the mirror at my hair that's a wild mess on top of my head. That's when I notice the hickey on my neck.

"Oh my God," I whisper, moving closer to the mirror. "A hickey?"

I hear low chuckling from the doorway where Levi is standing. My eyes dart to him in the reflection, and I can't help but notice how his joggers hang low on his hips.

I move my neck to the side, pointing at the mark on my neck. "Look what you did!"

Levi moves forward and stands behind me to get a closer view. Dipping down, he licks my neck and gently sucks. "I like marking you as mine."

Turning until I face him, I look up into his eyes. "I have to go back to work next week, sir. I can't have deep purple bruises on my neck like a teenager."

Leaning in, he slides his mouth across my lips, leaving me nearly breathless. "Didn't hear you complaining last night."

He breaks his hold on me.

"I'm going to kick your ass," I warn, meeting his gaze in the mirror.

"I welcome it, sweetheart."

Shaking my head, I walk out of the bathroom and go downstairs for coffee. Levi lets Dasher out and sits at the breakfast nook.

"Can I cook for you?" I ask.

He nearly looks shocked. "Sure."

"If I fuck it up, we can trash it," I say, pulling eggs, spinach, ham, and cheese from the fridge.

"I'd eat it with a smile," he quips.

"Even if it was burnt and as hard as a rock?"

He ponders my question for a moment. "No. If Dasher won't eat it, then neither will I."

With a snicker, I pour some oil into the pan. It's nearly impossible to mess up an omelet, but I have before. This time, though, I take my time, focusing on the eggs and sliding it on a plate when I think it's good.

Grabbing a fork, I set it down in front of Levi, eagerly waiting.

He cuts into it, pops a bite into his mouth, and hums. "If I had known you cooked this great, I'd have put you on breakfast duty weeks ago."

"You're just saying that."

"I swear," he says as I turn and make mine. By the time I join him, he's finished eating, but he keeps me company.

"So what do you have planned today?" he asks.

"Nothing much. I want to try to work for a few hours and call my sister at some point."

"And this evening?"

I take another bite. "You're the only thing on my to-do list later."

"Great. Well, I'm going to let you get some work done. I need to run to town. Do you need anything?"

I shake my head. "Not that I can think of."

Levi stands, pressing his lips against my neck. "Leave the dishes in the sink. I'll clean up when I get back."

"Thank you," I tell him as he goes upstairs to change.

After I'm done eating and Levi has left, I grab my laptop and log in to my email. Excitement rushes through me when I see several replies from my boss. I read his messages as fast as I can and let out a happy yelp.

I think this might be your best work to date. It's intriguing. I'm looking forward to reading more.

The pride that I feel has me reeling. I check the message from the senior editor and look at all the suggestions she made for me on the first few pages. I'll have to rework some things, but I know it's going to be so much stronger. For the first time since I started at the magazine, I'm actually excited for my work to be published. If the right people read it, my career could skyrocket.

I think about where the rest of the story is going and make a few notes, then decide to let those ideas marinate for a little while. Once I check the time and notice it's not too early in Seattle, I decide to FaceTime my sister.

She answers on the third ring and grins wide.

"Look at you!" Taryn says, then she puts her face closer to the screen. "Wait, is that a hickey on your neck?"

I lift my shirt, trying to cover it, completely forgetting about it. "Shit."

"It is! Oh my God. Spill the tea, girl."

A big smile fills my face. "He's amazing."

She squeals. "Like amazing, you want to have a million babies with him, and move to Vermont amazing?"

"Uh. Slow down. Amazing like I'm happy and am just seeing where this goes because we haven't talked about what will happen when I leave."

She makes a face. "What? Why?"

"We both know I'm leaving and are enjoying each other while we can. That way there's no pressure. Doesn't mean it's the end of the world."

"Did you fall and hit your head or something?" Taryn asks.

"No. I'm just trying not to get my heart broken," I admit, sucking in a deep breath.

"Well, I support whatever you decide," Taryn tells me. "My mom's group has still been asking about your relationship, though. Might have to give them a juicy update."

"Gah, Taryn. Why don't you just write a book about it and use me as character inspiration?"

Her eyes light up with excitement. "That is the perfect idea. And apparently writing runs in the family."

I snicker. "I'll be your number one fan."

"You better," she tells me. "Because I'm gonna tell everyone it's my little sister's love story."

I laugh out loud. "You better not."

"I can do whatever I want," she teases, and we both smile wide. "Thanks for calling me today."

"Always, sis. I love you so much."

"I love you, too, Fallon. Please take care of yourself," she says.

"I always do," I tell her. The back door opens, and Dasher gets up and runs toward Levi, who's carrying at least ten bags of groceries. "I should probably let you go," I tell her.

"Okie dokie! Have fun banging the hot lumberjack," she says, and I try to turn her down, but Levi bursts into laughter.

"Bye," I say between gritted teeth and end the call.

"Shoulda let me chat with her," he says.

"Oh, God no. I'm not stupid. My sister would embarrass the fire out of me."

"Damn, missing my opportunity." He snaps his fingers.

"Need any help?" I ask, shutting my laptop, knowing I'm pretty much done for the day. I walk into the kitchen and see all the ingredients he's taking out of the bags.

"What are we baking?" I ask.

"Gingersnaps," he explains, and I search his eyes.

"But it's a secret."

"Yes. But these will be slightly different because I'm making them gluten-free, so technically *not* the same. After we make them, though, you're sworn to secrecy for life."

"So I guess that means no publishing it in the magazine?"

Levi growls. "Woman."

"I'm kidding. I'd never do that. I'm actually more scared of your mom being disappointed than any punishment you'd give me."

He lifts his brows. "As you should be."

I look at the coconut flour, ginger, cinnamon, salt, and baking soda. Then there's this weird jar of something that doesn't have a label.

"What's this?" I ask, picking it up, studying how thick it is.

"That's the secret ingredient." He takes it from my hand and sets it down on the counter. "Don't drop it."

"Can we make these now?" I ask, more intrigued than anything. But also, I love those cookies.

"Are you done for the day?" he asks as he grabs some butter and eggs from the fridge.

"I am now," I say, washing my hands after Levi. "Teach me your ways."

Levi grabs a mixing bowl and spoon and hands it to me. "Ready?"

I enthusiastically nod, then he picks up the coconut flour and pours it in the bowl.

"You're not measuring anything?" I look at him like he's lost his mind.

"Why would I?" He snickers, adding more baking soda, cinnamon, and salt.

I scoff. "Because I'm supposed to be learning!"

He shakes his head and wraps his hand around my waist, pulling me into him. "You learn by doing, naughty girl."

"You're evil," I say as he slides his tongue into my mouth.

When we break apart, he grabs another bowl.

"Mix the powders," he directs, turning on the oven. "You know what the real secret of these cookies are? The reason Finn can never get them right?"

I meet his eyes.

"It's because he's trying to imitate something that comes straight from the heart. The recipe lives up here." He points at his head. "And here." Then his heart.

"You can't replicate that," I whisper.

"No," Levi confirms as he whips butter and cracks eggs.

Once we've mixed the dry and wet ingredients, we roll the dough in our hands, then we place them a few inches apart on the tray. Levi puts them in the oven and sets a timer for eight minutes.

"You know what that means?"

I shake my head.

"I have eight minutes to make you come," he tells me, scooping me up into his arms and carrying me to the living room. Dasher barely lifts his head from where he's lying in front of the fire.

Levi sets me down on the couch and slides my pajama bottoms and panties down. He spreads my legs, diving headfirst between my thighs, and I writhe against him. He licks, sucks, and finger fucks me into oblivion as I tug on his hair.

"Shit," I whisper-hiss, as he curves his finger, hitting my G-spot. As my eyes slam shut, the orgasm builds. I moan out his name as he flicks his tongue against my clit, and soon, I'm spilling over. He laps up my arousal, then slides his mouth down my thighs, kissing them too. Before he stands, the timer on the oven dings.

"Cookies are done," he says, smirking.

I catch my breath, then meet him in the kitchen. When he pulls the tray out, he slams it against the oven, and I jump.

"Why'd you do that?"

"Makes the middle of the dough fall flat and makes all the cracks happen on top."

I look at them with amazement. "When can we eat them?"

"Gotta let them cool, so about fifteen minutes?"

I bite the corner of my lip.

"Perfect." I grab his hand and lead us back to the couch, wanting to return the favor. "That's all the time I need."

CHAPTER TWENTY-TWO

LEVI

DAY 27

IT's the day I've been dreading, but it's unavoidable.

For the past week, we've spent as much time together as we could, baking cookies, drinking hard cider, snuggling by the fire, and making love. It's been a perfect bubble that's about to burst.

Fallon stirs next to me as I hold her against my chest. My palm rubs over her back, wandering down her spine to her ass. Everything about her is perfect, and I hate that I have to let her leave today.

I'd get on my knees and beg her to stay if I thought she actually would. She has to return to her life and job in Seattle, and although we could try a long-distance relationship, neither of us has mentioned it. We both know it probably wouldn't work given that she travels, and I can't leave Dasher or be away from the farm for weeks at a time. It's my life, and leaving my family would be impossible.

This is what we agreed to, and I have to respect it, even if I'm dying inside.

"I never wanna get out of this bed," she murmurs as she inches closer.

I smile at her words, nodding in agreement.

"Me neither, but we have to."

"Just five more minutes," she pleads, squeezing her arm tighter around me.

I can't deny her that, so I stay put.

"Do you think Dasher will wonder where I am?" she asks moments later, sadness coating her voice.

"Probably. He got used to your shit-talking."

She chuckles. "My clothes are gonna be full of his hair forever."

"Welcome to being a dog parent where you vacuum three times a week."

"I wish I was home enough to have a pet."

"What about a fish?"

She snorts. "They still have to be fed. But I'd probably find a way to kill it, trust me."

"You could get a cat. They have automatic litter boxes, along with food and water wells. That way you wouldn't have to worry about it for like ten days."

"I'd feel guilty leaving it alone that long."

"That's how I feel about Dasher when I have to work long days and can't bring him with me. I just imagine him having the best naps and not giving a shit I'm gone."

She laughs, then leans up to look at me. "Can't believe I'm saying this, but I'm gonna miss that fur ball. And his hot owner, too."

I wrap a piece of hair around her ear and rub the pad of my thumb over her cheek. "His owner is gonna miss you as well."

Tears swell in the corner of her eyes, and I catch one before it falls. "Let me make you some coffee and breakfast before you leave."

"I'd like that. I have to finish packing and take a shower."

I kiss her forehead. "Perfect, I'll have it ready by the time you're out."

I'm tempted to roll her over and devour her one last time, but we spent yesterday evening saying goodbye for hours. There were so many times I wanted to tell her how my heart was aching, and that my house would forever feel empty with her gone.

But that wouldn't help either of us.

We're both already sad as hell that this is ending, so I don't need to drive the knife deeper.

Just as we crawl out of bed, Dasher comes in and jumps on the mattress. "C'mon, let's go outside," I tell him, and he sprints downstairs. I quickly put on some joggers and grab a T-shirt, but then notice which one it is.

"Fallon." I turn around and show her the same T-shirt she wore the day I caught her in my bathtub. "You should keep this."

"Are you sure?"

"Yeah. It looks better on you anyway." I shoot her a wink. "Plus, I have an endless supply."

She grabs it and presses it to her nose. "It smells like you."

"My entire house smells like *you*." I smirk.

Dasher barks from downstairs, and I groan. "Meet you in the kitchen," I tell her, then press my lips to hers.

As soon as my foot hits the bottom step, Dasher runs in circles. "Go take your zoomies outside." I open the door, and he flies off the deck. I leave it cracked so he can come back in when he's ready. I want to make sure I have enough time to cook Fallon something to eat before she has to make her long journey home.

We went grocery shopping a few days ago, but I still have some of the weird foods she hasn't eaten, so I'll have to see if my sister wants it. It'll only be a reminder that she's really gone.

I start her coffee and get her favorite mug ready. Once she's done with it today, I plan to clean it and give it to her because I know how much she likes the farm logo on it.

"Something smells good." She comes down, looking pretty as always in black leggings, boots, and a sweater. Her long locks are pulled up in a messy bun, and her face is freshly cleaned from her shower. Fallon's gorgeous whether she's dressed up or down, but I especially love this look on her. Casual and cute.

"Come eat while it's hot," I say.

She drinks her coffee and eats her turkey bacon. Dasher sits next to her, begging for some. I refill his water and food quickly so he stops slobbering on her.

"Got everything packed?" I ask, wiping off the counters.

"Yep. Not looking forward to unpacking or doing laundry, though."

"Yeah, that's always the downside to traveling."

"Luckily, I did a couple of loads here, so I won't have as much to do when I get home. I'm gonna need a couple of days to adjust to the time difference before I have to repack for my next assignment."

At the mention of where she's going next, I frown. She's told me about it, and I'm happy she's getting to do something she'll enjoy, but she'll be three thousand miles away from me.

"At least you'll get to drink lots of coffee," I remind her.

"That's true. I'll probably be wired the whole time." She laughs softly.

"I'm sure the article will turn out great."

"That reminds me. Do you want to give me your email so I can send you the final article before it goes to publication? It'll be a few weeks until it's ready."

"You're gonna actually let me read it?" I arch a brow, and she rolls her eyes.

"Of course. I want you to like it."

I smile. "It's Levi@Whiteschristmastreefarm.com."

"Okay, perfect, I'll put that in my phone so I don't forget. My boss is already begging to read the final, but I still need to fine-tune it."

"Everyone in town is looking forward to it, too."

"So...no pressure?" She sighs.

I spin her chair until she faces me, and I can stand between her legs. "They wouldn't have sent you here if they didn't think you could do it justice. I have full confidence in your ability to make this article the absolute best that it can be."

"You have too much faith in me."

"None of that self-doubt, my love." I lift her chin and press my lips to hers. "Finish your coffee, and I'll load up your bags in your *sweet* minivan and get it started for ya."

She laughs, pushing me away. "That beast got me here in one piece, so be nice."

Dasher follows me around as I grab her bags and carry them outside. It's cold and sunny, the complete opposite of the day she arrived, so she should have no problem getting to the airport today. I would've loved to have driven her there myself.

Once I'm inside, I clean out her mug and dry it off. "I want you to have this," I tell her. "Take a piece of Vermont back with you."

"Why are you trying to make me cry? I hate crying." She sniffs, grabbing it from my hand.

I pull her into my chest, holding her tight as she forces back tears. She's not the only one, though. My emotions are about to spill over.

"Before you go, I need to say something."

She leans back and meets my eyes.

"Finding you in my house has been the greatest thing to ever happen to me. You will forever have a piece of my heart, Fallon Joy. Regardless of where our lives take us, I'l never forget our time together. I want the absolute best for you and hope all your dreams come true. You deserve it and so much more."

My own tears fall, blurring my vision as I feel her moist cheeks against my fingers.

"You suck, and I really dislike you for making me cry." She choke-laughs as she tries to compose herself.

"It's okay to show emotion, sweetheart. It's not a weakness." I kiss her again. "Just don't tell *my* sister I cried."

"I'm going to miss her and your family, too. Finn and Oakley. Everyone. Even the mayor who dresses like Santa."

"It took a while, but I think we finally got you hooked on our little town," I say with amusement.

"It's the community. You were right from the beginning. It's the people who make this place so special and magical."

"It's going to be a little less special without you here," I tell her honestly.

"Thank you for...*everything*. You helped give me holiday memories I can cherish forever. When sadness takes over, I'll have them to hold on to."

"I'm happy to hear that." I take her hand and walk her outside. If she doesn't leave soon, she'll miss her flight.

Dasher wags his tail, and she kneels to give him a hug. "I'm gonna miss you, buddy, even though you suck at listening to me. You were a good snuggler."

I beam as I watch Dasher lick her face.

Once she stands, I take her into my arms one final time.

"My house is always open to you, Fallon."

She nods as she fights back tears.

Then I open her van door, and she gets in, setting her phone in the middle and buckling. It's nice and warm for her, too.

Leaning against the frame, I dip down and capture her mouth. Our tongues tangle in a heated war of all the words we can't say. Cupping her face, I deepen our kiss and moan. She does the same, and I hate that I'll never hear it again.

When we're breathless, I pull back. "Drive safe, okay?"

"I will. Thank you again for letting me crash here."

"Don't mention it." I shoot her a wink.

"Bye." The sadness in her voice is a punch to the gut.

"See ya, Fallon Joy."

Dasher and I watch as she rolls down the driveway, and I wave one last time before she's completely out of view.

"She's gone now, buddy. Come inside," I tell him as I walk up the steps, but he's frozen in place. "Dasher! Inside."

He keeps watching as if he's waiting for her to come back. My heart was already breaking, but now it's shattered, knowing he got attached, too.

When I reach the door, I whistle, and he finally listens.

As soon as I walk into the living room, I feel her loss.

It's empty and cold.

The farm is closed for New Year's Day, so I can't even work to keep my mind busy. Instead, I'll lie in bed and soak up the last remaining memories we made together.

CHAPTER TWENTY-THREE

LEVI

THREE WEEKS LATER

IT'S BEEN radio silence from Fallon since she texted to let me know she made it home—*three weeks ago*.

We never discussed staying in contact. Honestly, it'd only allow the pain from missing her so much to linger. But damn, I wish I could talk to her.

I'm not the only one suffering. Dasher lies exclusively on the side of the couch where she'd sit, and he took over her spot on the bed.

A week ago, I snapped and looked her up on social media. She's posted a few pictures of the Vermont landscapes and even one of Dasher, which I thought was adorable as hell. Then I fixated on the selfies from the past year, and she's gorgeous in every shot. Based on the photographs she's posted over the years, she's well traveled. How anyone could break up with her is beyond me.

I'd never consider myself a love-sick puppy type of guy, but apparently, I am for her. At least I can stare at images of her.

"It's giving me *stalker vibes*." I can almost hear her voice in my head now and smile.

There are a few recent ones of the coffee roasters she's visited, and she looks happy.

Work is always slow after the holidays, which I would normally appreciate and enjoy, but right now, I need something to keep my mind busy. I've even resorted to asking Lucy to let me work with her in the gift shop. She ecstatically agreed.

After two hours of her drilling me about Fallon, I gave up and left.

My mom's told me half a dozen times to fly to Seattle and surprise her. As soon as Lucy heard about Mom's idea, she jumped on board and kept saying how *romantic* it'd be. Immediately, I told them no, but after thinking about it, I booked a flight and hotel.

I plan to call her once I get there since I don't know her exact address. Hopefully, she's home, so I can tell her how I've fallen in love with her. It'll either be the beginning of us or the closure we need. I never understood the phrase *right person, wrong time* until I met Fallon.

If she says she can't do long distance, then I'll kiss her one last time and walk away for good.

My phone rings, and I put it on speaker. "What, Lucy?"

"Am I still driving you to the airport tomorrow?"

"Yes," I confirm. "Six o'clock."

"Oh my God, that's so early," she groans.

"Suck it up. This idea was partly yours," I remind her, though I'm not mad about it.

"I'm so excited for you. Have you packed?"

"I am right now, *Mom*."

"Did you stock the fridge and pantry for me?"

"Of course."

"Perfect! Dasher and I are gonna have a blast," she says with a smile in her voice. Since I'll be gone for seven days, I asked Lucy to house-sit and watch Dasher.

"No being nosy and snooping through my room." I know my sister too damn well.

"Yeah, yeah. Oh, before I forget. Mom emailed a work thing you're supposed to read and sign."

"Okay, I'll check once I'm done putting my shit in this bag."

"Alrighty. See ya tomorrow, little brother!"

She hangs up before I can remind her we're only two minutes apart. Little brat.

I grab my laptop, then walk downstairs with Dasher following. Since I'm not taking it with me, I clear out my mail.

I find the one Lucy's talking about and read it over. Then I delete all the junk that's been collecting for the past month.

Just as I'm about to exit out of the window, a new email pops up, and the sender's name grabs my attention.

Fallon Joy.

The subject is: **Finding the Christmas Spirit in Vermont's North Pole**

The smile on my face widens at her choice of title.

I click it open.

Levi White,
This is scheduled to be published next week. I hope it's to your liking.
-Fallon Joy

I frown at her formal message.

That's it, huh?

I download the attachment and get comfortable on the couch. This piece will either make or break our special town.

I'm impressed by how long and in-depth it is. Her opening paragraph has me laughing when she mentions hating the cold, and her descriptions of the blizzard and living without amenities make me smile at those memories. Given the storm's severity, she highlighted how fast the crews cleared the roads and restored power. She goes on to discuss her time snowed in, and then she introduces me and my family's tree farm.

Levi White and his family's Christmas tree farm is a town staple, and it's no surprise why. Whether you want to chop down your own tree or choose one that's ready to go, the experience will be filled with family-friendly fun. While you wait for your tree with a homemade hot cocoa in hand, you can enjoy numerous other activities, such as horse-drawn sleigh rides, a gift shop with a wrapping station, and the best gingersnap cookies I've ever had. Whether you enjoy visiting old friends or meeting new ones, there's plenty of room for everyone. With festive music playing around the farm, you'll never be without the Christmas spirit. Take it from someone who hasn't celebrated the holidays in over a decade, White's Christmas Tree Farm is a holiday tradition you won't want to miss!

Every word I read has me smiling wider.

She really wrote each word with heart and non-biases.

I continue reading with pride at how highly she speaks of our town, the locals, and the community. Then she spotlights the small businesses that work hard to offer quality items. The section on the ski resort will be wonderful for their business.

The feature on Bennett's Orchard Farms is amazing. Finn and his family will be pleased, and I hope it brings in even more tourists during the fall season. She speaks nothing but praise and talks about the history along with last year's centennial celebration. Although she wasn't here for it, they had tons of photos to show her.

She even mentions Oakley, the town's famous painter, and how her artwork is featured throughout the town. I chuckle, knowing how much she'll love that.

Mayor Myers gets his own mention as she ties in some of the history he shared with her.

By the end, she's giving our town her highest recommendation. She encourages families to visit during the winter so they can spend quality time together and hypes it as the perfect romantic getaway for couples.

Then I read the last paragraph.

I'll leave you with my final thoughts.
Find someone who makes you become a better version of yourself and if
you're lucky enough to find that person, never let them go. I arrived in
Vermont wanting nothing to do with Christmas and all that comes with it.
By the end, I'd left a piece of my heart there. They managed to take
someone who's nicknamed The Grinch and make her fall in love again—
with Christmas and everything that revolves around it.

I'm hardly breathing by the time I finish.

On top of it being beautifully written, this only validates my decision to see her.

I can't wait to thank her in person.

Another email pops up, but it's from her personal account, with the subject line: **Read After**

Levi,

I hope you enjoyed the article and wanted you to know that I meant every single word. While I was there, I met a lot of special people who I'll never forget. But by far, you're the most important person I've met, not only during this trip but in my entire life. You've helped me more than you'll ever realize.

You helped me see that it's okay to enjoy Christmas again, the way my mother would've wanted me to.

You helped me understand that not everyone has bad intentions when it comes to love and dating, and showed me what I truly deserve.

You helped me find myself again after feeling lost for longer than I want to admit.

And most importantly, you helped me realize that a rare kind of love like ours is worth fighting for.

Sorry for dropping the L-bomb in an email, but I couldn't wait to tell you. Every day we spent together, I fell harder for you. Leaving you and Dasher was more painful than I realized it would be. I wish I could've stayed with you, but I made a commitment to my boss, and I wanted to fulfill that.

It wasn't until two weeks later that I realized my job would never make me as happy as you do.

So after my coffee roasters article, I sent in my resignation letter.

My boss was just as shocked as I was, but I don't regret it. In fact, I feel elated and free. Like I can finally go anywhere and do anything. Travel and see the world without a journalist's eye and just...live.

I was drowning in guilt and lived in the past, but with your help, I've realized it's time to take charge of my life again.

And I really need to thank you for teaching me that even as an adult, it's okay to have snowball fights, make snow angels, ski down bunny hills, and laugh until I cry.

Levi White, you've changed my life, and I'll love you forever because of that.
-Fallon

PS—I sent something to your house. It should be there now.

It takes a few moments to wipe my face and clear my vision. She has no idea how much I needed that, and now I get to tell her tomorrow in person that I love her too.

Dasher lays his head on my arm as if he knows Fallon wrote us.

"Don't worry, she mentioned you too." I pet him, but he starts whining. "What's wrong?"

He barks and jumps off of the couch, spinning around. He's losing his damn mind pacing and yelping.

"Okay, relax! Dasher! Chill out. Let's go outside."

At that mention, he bolts toward the door, and when I open it, my jaw drops.

FALLON

Where the hell is he?

I'm freezing my ass off on Levi's deck.

Why did I think this was a good idea?

Oh right, I'm trying to be romantic, and well, right now, it feels like a whole lot of bullshit.

What's taking him so long?

I know he read my email fifteen minutes ago when I peeked into his front window.

And yes, that makes me sound like the *obsessive murder-y* type, but I tried to time this perfectly, and he's ruining it.

Time for plan B.

I brought a dog whistle just in case I needed a little help from Dasher. Here goes nothing.

When I blow it, Dasher barks. Then I do it until I hear his paws dancing across the hardwood flooring. I suppress a laugh when Levi yells for him to chill out. My heart races when the shuffling of his feet comes closer.

Finally.

Dasher will get all the treats for being the goodest boy.

"Okay, relax! Dasher! Chill out. Let's go outside."

When Levi opens the door, Dasher immediately spots me and jumps up. Levi's eyes widen.

"Fallon?"

"Hey." I smile, trying to push Dasher off me.

"Wh-What are you doing here?" Levi asks, shocked.

"Getting frostbite, apparently."

"Jesus. Come inside." He grabs my hand and pulls me in, then shuts the door behind us. "Your face is so cold." He cups my cheeks, and I lean into his warmth.

"You took forever reading my email," I murmur. "In hindsight, I should've just knocked."

"Fuck, I'm sorry. I got a little emotional, and then Dasher lost his shit."

I hold up the whistle and smirk. "I needed his help."

He shakes his head with amusement. "So you really quit your job?"

"Yep. Handed in my last assignment yesterday and flew in this morning."

"I can't believe you're here." Our mouths crash together, and he twists his tongue with mine. "I've missed you so fucking much."

"I missed you too," I tell him as he presses his forehead to mine. "I couldn't walk away from the love of my life."

He pulls back.

"Dasher," I confirm, and he bursts out laughing.

"That little bastard stole my woman."

I chuckle. "No, I'm all yours. That's if...you'll have me?"

"Fallon, I'm *crazy* about you."

"I wasn't sure if surprising you would be inconvenient or—" I tilt my head when I notice the suitcases by the door. "Oh, are you going somewhere?"

He grins, scrubbing a hand through his hair. "Well, I *was*."

"I'm sorry. I should've called. Just showing up sounds romantic in the movies, but—"

He closes the gap between us and takes my mouth again. "Baby, I was going to see you."

"What? You were?"

"Before I got your emails, I had everything planned. Lucy was going to watch Dasher. I took off work for a week. I even bought one of those neck pillows so I could sleep on the plane."

I snort, shaking my head in disbelief.

"Well, it's a good thing I came today because there wouldn't have been an apartment for you to visit me in. I moved out."

"Good, because now that I have you here, I'm not letting you go." He lifts me until my legs wrap around his waist. "Your article is brilliant, by the way. You're a talented writer."

"I'm happy you liked it." I bring my lips back to his. "I hope everyone else does."

"They will."

He walks us into the living room and sits on the couch with my thighs straddling him. I remove my coat and hat, then wrap my arms around his neck. Before I can kiss him again, he cups my cheek.

"You have no idea how hard I've fallen for you. Having you back in my arms is a dream come true," he says so sweetly, then kisses the tip of my nose.

"I couldn't live with myself if I let the best thing that's ever happened to me get away. Falling for you was unexpected, but I can't imagine my life without you in it."

"I'm so in love with you, Fallon. You have no idea how much you've impacted my life." Dasher jumps on the couch and licks my face. "His too, apparently."

We laugh as I give him much-earned attention. Finally, he gets down and lies on the floor.

"My family will freak when they find out," he says. "Especially Lucy."

"Maybe we don't tell them right away?" I bite my lip with a mischievous grin. "Well, you can tell your sister so she doesn't barge in on something she'll regret seeing."

He arches a brow with a devious smirk as if he likes where this conversation is going.

"We could stay locked up here for the next week and make up for lost time," I suggest, and by his erection poking into me, I know he's on board.

"You're so naughty." He smacks my ass, grinding me harder against him.

I smile wide. "That's why you love me."

"So goddamn much."

Our lips fuse as he pulls off my shirt, then unsnaps my bra. I turn and look at Dasher who's staring at us.

"Bedroom," I mutter, and he immediately agrees.

He carries me over his shoulder, and I squeal for him to put me down.

"Don't think my possessive mountain man ways have changed since you left."

"Damn you." I chuckle.

Once he sets me on the bed, I lie back, and he towers over me. "I'm spending every minute of the next seven days inside you. Hope you're ready."

"You're gonna have to caffeinate and feed me at some point," I tease.

"Okay, deal. But for right now, I'm not waiting another second."

He strips off his clothes, then removes the rest of mine. "Spread those legs for me, my love," he demands as he strokes his thick cock, staring between my thighs. "Fuck, you're perfect."

Levi kneels on the bed and positions himself at my entrance, teasing my clit with his crown. "Let me hear you say those words again."

"Which ones?"

"That you love me."

"I just flew three thousand miles for you," I retort.

With a small thrust, he goes in one inch. "Say. The. Words. Fallon."

Smirking, I reach down and play with my clit. "I. Love. You." I repeat his emphasis on each word but also want to make sure he truly understands how much he means to me. "But if you don't *fuck me* right this minute, I'm going to scream."

"Don't worry, baby. You'll still be screaming."

Then he pushes all the way inside, and I gasp at the tight intrusion. "God, yes."

"Are you on birth control?" he asks, and I'm slightly taken aback by the timing of his question.

"Isn't that something you should've asked over a month ago?" I breathe out between his movements.

"Probably." He laughs, slowing his pace. "But I used a condom the first time, and then I always pulled out after. So that's why I need to know now."

I worry he's going to be mad but answer him honestly. "No. The hormones always messed with me, and I got tired of trying new ones."

"Fuck, explain to me why that makes me want to knock you up right now."

I beam at the thought. "Do it."

He arches a brow as if he wasn't expecting that response.

"I'd love nothing more than to have a family with you," I confirm.

"Goddamn, woman. You just unleashed something feral inside me, and now that I'm on a mission, I won't stop until we succeed."

I chuckle. "You and your missions are what got us here."

He buries his cock in deeper as he kisses my neck and groans in my ear. "You're so perfect for me, baby. So damn smart, beautiful, and witty. I still can't believe you're here."

"I'm never leaving you again," I promise, wrapping my arms around him.

"Good, because just know, next time, I *will* chase you."

I laugh, then bite down on my bottom lip because at any second, I'll explode. "Make me come, *please*. I'm so close."

"Hold on tight. I'm about to put a baby inside you."

As soon as he says those words, my legs shake, and pleasure shoots down my body. I moan out his name and claw at his back, and he buries his face in my neck and sucks hard.

"*One*," I say unprompted.

His lips turn up into a pleased grin. "Such a good girl."

My cheeks heat, loving his praise.

"With what I have planned for you this week, you'll be counting much higher than that. But this time, I need you right now."

"*Yes, please.*"

"I hope you were serious about the baby thing. Otherwise, you better speak up."

Instead of answering, I lock my ankles behind his back and dig my fingers into his arms. He's not going anywhere.

"Fuck," he growls.

Moments later, he's filling me full, giving me everything and more.

"I can't wait to see you pregnant with my baby." He kisses me.

"Me too. Dasher will make a great big brother," I say as we breathlessly lie next to each other.

"I agree." He pulls me into him, then covers us with the blankets.

"I love you," I whisper once we've caught our breaths.

"I love you so much." He rests his palm on my belly. "And our child."

I chuckle. "Getting a little ahead, aren't we?"

"Never. If you thought I was possessive over you before, just wait."

I playfully roll my eyes. We lie in bed for hours, snuggling and talking about our future. For the first time, I'm actually looking forward to next Christmas. We could be parents by then and make our own family holiday traditions.

Something I never knew I wanted until I met Levi.

EPILOGUE
LEVI

TEN MONTHS LATER

As I WAIT at the altar next to my best friend, I look over at my beautiful wife standing on the other side and smile at her swollen belly with pride. Getting to be a part of Finn and Oakley's wedding party has been super special, and walking down with my wife made it even better.

Her being nearly nine months along has made summer interesting. We spent most of it getting the nursery ready and helping our friends plan their fall-themed orchard wedding. It's been the best year of my life, and I can't wait to see what the rest of it brings.

At the sound of "Canon in D" playing, everyone stands, and we watch Oakley make her way down the aisle. I put my hand on Finn's shoulder, giving him an encouraging squeeze since he hasn't turned around yet.

"She looks stunning," I whisper.

He taps my hand back with the biggest smile I've ever seen on his face.

I glance over at Fallon again. We officially got married seven months ago at the courthouse but had a small ceremony and reception four months later at the tree farm. It was the first time her family visited although I met them in April when we flew to Seattle for Easter. It was great showing them around the farm and town.

When Finn finally turns around and sees his bride, he immediately chokes up. Oakley's a ball of emotions, fighting back tears as she wipes under her eyes. These two couldn't be more perfect for each other.

The officiant begins the ceremony, and by the end, there isn't a dry eye in the audience. Their vows were sweet and personal. There's nothing better than seeing my best friend get his happily ever after.

"My feet are killing me," Fallon whispers as we wait for the photographer to finish. We did a million group shots, and now they're taking separate family ones.

"Take off your shoes," I tell her.

"I can't reach." She pouts. "Can you help me?"

Chuckling, I kneel and motion for her to lift her foot. "Jesus. These things need a passcode or something to untie?"

"Don't look at me. Oakley picked out these hand-sewn laced up the ankle killer traps."

I finally manage to get one off, then reach for her other.

"Oh shit," Fallon blurts out, leaning on my shoulder.

"What's wrong?" I panic, standing and holding her shoulders.

"The contractions are getting stronger." She squeezes her eyes and blows out a long breath.

"You're in labor?"

"I thought it was just Braxton Hicks, but they've been consistent for the past hour."

"Baby, we have to get you to the hospital," I urge.

"No, no, I'm fine. Contractions can last hours, and I don't wanna ruin —" She screams as she leans against me.

"Yeah, we're going. Right now."

"What's the matter?" Tatum, Oakley's sister, comes over to help.

"I'm taking her to the hospital. She's in labor."

"Give me your keys, and I'll get your truck," Tatum says, springing into action.

I dig in my pocket and hand them over. "It's parked on the east side."

"Be right back."

"Just breathe, baby. You've got this."

Since we're in the orchard, there's nowhere to sit. Finally, Finn and Oakley return with the photographer.

"Oh my God, is she okay?" Finn rushes over.

"I'm fine, just about to have a baby in the woods is all."

I shake my head at her dramatics. "It's not the woods, sweetheart. And you're not having him now."

"How far apart are your contractions?" Oakley asks.

"I'm not sure. It was around twenty minutes a few hours ago, and now they're—"

"Argh, fuck." Fallon hunches over, but I hold her up as best I can.

"I think they're at five minutes now," I tell her.

"Shit, I hope you make it in time," she says. The hospital's thirty minutes away.

"Your son better not make me give birth outside without an epidural," Fallon hisses, holding her stomach as if she's trying to keep him pushed inside.

"He's a White. He's gonna do what he wants," Finn says with a light chuckle, and Fallon rewards him with a glare.

Finally, tires squeal, and I see my truck approaching. "Let's go, baby."

"No speeding," Oakley demands.

Yeah, right.

Finn helps me get her into the passenger side, and once Fallon's secure, I rush around to the driver's side.

"Keep us updated!" Oakley shouts, and I nod.

Once I'm buckled, I gun it out of there.

FALLON
Four Hours Later

"Nicholas Kane White, you stubborn little boy." I rub the pad of my thumb over his chubby cheek and smile at the beautiful baby they claim is mine. How the hell I pushed out a ten-pounder is beyond me, but thank God for painkillers. He was so big that his head got stuck, and the doctor had to use forceps to pull him out.

I'm pretty sure I'm never having sex again.

"So when can we make another?" Levi asks as if he didn't just watch my vagina stretch out to accommodate a human head.

I shoot him a murderous glare.

"What? He needs a sister." He smirks.

"Dasher and Rudy already keep us plenty busy. Now, it's gonna be three against two," I tell him. A few months ago, we added a golden retriever puppy to the chaos. We hoped it'd help Dasher get acquainted with having a baby around, and they play-wrestle all day, but I'm constantly tripping over the toys they leave out.

"We'll figure it out, my love. What's life without a little chaos?"

I chuckle, hoping I can handle it all. Ever since I moved here, I've taken on some freelance work, but I stopped a few months ago when the new puppy started taking up more of my time. Now I just help at the farm's gift shop when they need an extra hand.

"Finn and Oakley are here," I tell her.

"They left the reception?"

"Yeah, they couldn't wait to meet him."

"Aw. Well, tell them to come in, then."

Five minutes later, the bride and groom enter.

"He's so cute," Oakley gushes when she gets a good look at him. "Look at his chunky face."

"Looks just like Levi," Finn teases.

"He's going to be a strong lumberjack like his daddy," I say, smiling.

They take turns holding him, rocking him in the chair next to my bed. Oakley tells us about the reception and how they left after their first dance so they could be here.

"I hope you go back and enjoy your special day," I tell her.

"Don't worry, we will. I won't be drinking, but—" Her hand flies to her mouth, and my jaw drops.

"You're pregnant, aren't you?"

Her cheeks flush and I know without a doubt, that's a yes.

"We just found out," she quickly adds.

"Congrats, you two!" Levi pulls Finn in for a hug.

"Our kids will get to grow up together." I smile at the thought.

"We better have a boy then," Finn says. "I don't trust a White around my little girl."

"*Oh God.*" I chuckle.

Oakley rolls her eyes. "And it begins."

We laugh and talk about all the exciting events we'll share together. She's due sometime in July before Nicholas turns one, so either way, we'll have lots of fun raising them together.

Levi's family comes in after Finn and Oakley leave, and when I'm ready to pass out, he makes everyone go. The pain meds they just gave me are making me drowsy.

"I'm going to take him to the nursery so you can get some sleep," Levi says, gently taking him from my arms.

I nod, too tired to even speak.

When Levi returns, he sits on the edge of my bed and brushes his hand over my cheek. "I'm so proud of you. Watching you give birth to our son was amazing."

I flash him a deadpan expression. "I'm glad you had fun," I mutter.

He chuckles. "That's why I love you so much."

I snort, too tired to even think of a comeback.

He pulls the covers up to my chest, tucking me in because he knows I hate being cold. "I'm going to lie in the bed next to yours. So let me know if you need anything or need me to find a nurse."

"Mm-hmm."

Leaning down, he presses his lips to my forehead. "Get some rest. Thank you for being the love of my life and giving me a family."

I force my eyes open and smile at my sweet husband. "Thank you for loving me when I needed it the most."

He takes my hand and kisses my knuckles. "You've been my greatest joy."

AVAILABLE NOW

If you haven't started the Love in Isolation series
from the beginning, read Elijah & Cameron's story
in *The Two of Us*

What happens when the entire world shuts down and you're quarantined in a cabin with your brother's best friend? You take every chance to make his life miserable, the same way he did yours, and most definitely don't fall in love.

The Two of Us is an enemies to lovers, brother's best friend standalone romance set in modern-day 2020.

ABOUT THE AUTHOR

Brooke Cumberland and Lyra Parish are a duo of romance authors who teamed up under the *USA Today* pseudonym, Kennedy Fox. They share a love of Hallmark movies, overpriced coffee, and making TikToks. When they aren't bonding over romantic comedies, they like to brainstorm new book ideas. One day in 2016, they decided to collaborate under a pseudonym and have some fun creating new characters that'll make you blush and your heart melt. Happily ever afters guaranteed!

CONNECT WITH US

Find us on our website:

kennedyfoxbooks.com

Subscribe to our newsletter:

kennedyfoxbooks.com/newsletter

facebook.com/kennedyfoxbooks

twitter.com/kennedyfoxbooks

instagram.com/kennedyfoxduo

amazon.com/author/kennedyfoxbooks

goodreads.com/kennedyfox

bookbub.com/authors/kennedy-fox

BOOKS BY KENNEDY FOX

DUET SERIES (BEST READ IN ORDER)

CHECKMATE DUET SERIES

ROOMMATE DUET SERIES

LAWTON RIDGE DUET SERIES

MOCKINGBIRD DUET

INTERCONNECTED STAND-ALONES

MAKE ME SERIES

BISHOP BROTHERS SERIES

CIRCLE B RANCH SERIES

LOVE IN ISOLATION SERIES

TEXAS HEAT SERIES

ONLY ONE SERIES

Find the entire Kennedy Fox reading order at
Kennedyfoxbooks.com/reading-order

Find all of our current freebies at
Kennedyfoxbooks.com/freeromance

CPSIA information can be obtained
at www.ICGtesting.com
Printed in the USA
BVHW031328100123
655986BV00002B/83